A

Lucy

Nazneen Sadiq

James Lorimer & Company, Publishers
Toronto, 1989

1-55028-238-7 paper   1-55028-239-5 cloth

Canadian Cataloguing in Publication Data

Sadiq, Nazneen, 1944-
Lucy
(Degrassi)
ISBN 1-55028-239-5 (bound)
ISBN 1-55028-238-7 (pbk.)
I. Title. II. Series.
PS8587.A3L8 1989   jC813'.54   C89-
095389-9
PZ7.S33Lu 1989

James Lorimer & Company, Publishers
Egerton Ryerson Memorial Building
35 Britain Street
Toronto, Ontario
M5A 1R7

Playing With Time Inc. acknowledges with thanks the writers — Yan Moore, Avrum Jacobson, Susin Nielsen, Kathryn Ellis — whose enthusiasm and dedication helped produce the original scripts on which this original story by Nazneen Sadiq is based.

CHAPTER 1

Lucy looked at herself in her bedroom mirror. She knew she was going to hate this term. She was also going to hate the month of February. Nothing was happening anywhere. Everything at Degrassi Junior High was a repetition of the same old thing. Who cared about graduation next term, if you died of boredom this term? She could barely keep from yawning in class. And she was getting fed up with her parents who kept flitting in and out of her life — mostly out. What was wrong with everybody, including herself? Even the new lip gloss she was applying so carefully was an old, blah colour. Something just has to happen to me, thought Lucy. She crammed the lip gloss into her school bag and headed for the kitchen.

Her mother was sitting at the dining table,

spooning chunks of grapefruit. She looked up at Lucy and made an awful face.

"Hello, baby. Never let yourself go, or you may have to suffer like this." Her mother tapped the grapefruit with the spoon.

Lucy gazed at her mother in exasperation. She was slim as a reed, but a couple of times a year she would go on her crazy grapefruit diet — just in case! Well, it was February and her mom was on her "just in case" binge. It was so predictable.

"How's school?" asked her mom. She spoke in that spacy, automatic way that made Lucy want to scream.

"It's no big deal," muttered Lucy.

"I'm going to be late tonight — I have a closing. Why don't you send out for a pizza?"

Lucy glanced at the twenty-dollar bill lying next to her place mat and shrugged her shoulders helplessly. She had been through this so often that she really didn't care anymore. Her mother sold real estate and was seldom around in the evenings. Her career was just beginning to take off, which meant that every time a house had to be sold she had to be there. A few more houses, Lucy, she would say, and then I can take it easy. So far, the few more houses had mush-roomed into lots more houses, and Lucy didn't believe anything her mother said anymore.

All this catch-up time in the morning was supposed to make it all right. It didn't. The awful part was that Lucy was supposed to be getting used to it. Getting older and managing on your own — that was the game. It was the hardest thing in the world for her, especially when she heard her friends at school talk about their evenings at home. That's when it mattered, because all of a sudden she was on the outside. But she had worked it out — by being cool about the whole subject. And she never wanted anyone to know that inside the cool person was somebody else. It was so much better to be admired by your friends than to be pitied.

"Lucy...." Her mom's voice was soft, almost apologetic. "Honey, I have a lot of deals going through this week. It's just a crazy time."

"It's okay," replied Lucy.

The telephone rang. Lucy watched her mother's attention shift, completely. It wasn't Mom sitting at the kitchen table, but a fast-talking stranger with words like "offer" and "mortgage" spilling out of her mouth. Lucy broke off pieces of banana muffin and squeezed them into hard little pellets. She didn't want any breakfast, and once again she had lost her mom. Some things never changed, thought Lucy miserably.

Why can't we all go back to New York, Lucy wondered. There her mother had treated her like a daughter, and not some sort of inconvenience that had to be shuffled around.

"I think I've got them," squeaked her mom, slamming down the phone. "Lucy, I've got to go. Don't forget to do your homework."

Lucy didn't even look at her mother. She tossed the pellets of banana muffin into the garbage and decided it was time to go to school. Maybe L.D. would get to school early and go over some of that stuff in Science. There was going to be a test and she had forgotten her textbook at school. Had she done it deliberately? Could she put one over on Mr. Garcia? He was such a fascist. They all were, except for that Mr. Colby. He was just a creep. All the bad dreams about Mr. Colby making a pass at her had gone. Still, a bit of a chill went through her whenever she thought of him. It was a rotten beginning for this boring day that would end with a boring pizza in the evening.

When Lucy reached school she couldn't find L.D.

"She has a doctor's appointment," said Heather.

"Lucky thing! She's going to miss the test." Erica rolled her eyes.

"Bye-bye, Science test," Lucy chanted.

"Lucy! Don't tell me you didn't study?" exclaimed Heather, looking horrified.

"Science is such a bore," Lucy shrugged.

"Is that a new lip gloss?" asked Erica.

"Yeah, but it's such a boring shade. Here, you want to try it?" Lucy dug it out of her bag.

"Do I want to try it?!" gurgled Erica.

Lucy and Heather watched Erica charge down the corridor towards the washroom just as the first period bell rang.

Mr. Garcia was waiting for them. Lucy took one look at his face and realized there wasn't any point in making excuses. She just didn't care enough. All she wanted to do was scribble something on the paper, hand it in and then escape to the washroom. But it wasn't that easy. Everyone else was hunched over the test with thoughtful looks on their faces. Mr. Garcia kept looking at her sternly. There was no way she could give him her cool, bored look back.

Why am I trapped here, Lucy thought to herself. She couldn't remember any of the stuff they had studied last week. Lucky L.D. — she would get an extra day to prepare for this wretched test.

Forty agonizing minutes later, when Lucy handed in her test papers to Mr. Garcia, he made it even worse.

"Lucy," he said, "I'm looking forward to an improvement from the last test."

For a moment Lucy felt as though she wanted to blurt something right back at him. I'm looking for an improvement too, she thought. I hate this draggy term. But she didn't say anthing. It would mean winding up in Mr. Lawrence's office.

"How did it go?" asked L.D. at lunch.

"It didn't," announced Lucy. "Who cares, anyway?"

"What's the matter with you?"

"I'm fed up. I wish I was someplace else."

"Yeah," said L.D. sympathetically, "I think I know what you mean."

"You don't have a clue, L.D."

"Sure I do. My dad's going kind of crazy these days." L.D. had a troubled expression in her eyes.

"Well, mine's disappeared somewhere over the horizon," muttered Lucy.

"I wouldn't mind trading places with you right now. It's doom and gloom at our place."

"Want to come over after school?" asked Lucy.

"I can't. My dad wants me close to home… in case…" L.D.'s voice trailed off.

6

"Okay, maybe tomorrow," shrugged Lucy. She hated the thought of spending another evening alone.

By the end of the afternoon, Lucy had decided she had had enough of school. It was crazy, because in the morning she had felt that she couldn't stand home. It was like being on a seesaw.

When Lucy opened the front door to her house she found a ton of flyers wedged behind the screen door. Her father hated junk mail, and used to toss everything into the garbage without looking at it. But once he had thrown out some papers for her mom, by accident. So now they had to sort it out.

It was going to be a long evening with her father out of town and her mom working. Lucy plonked the flyers on the kitchen table. She spread some raspberry jam on a croissant and munched it while she flipped through the flyers. It was all junky stuff except one coloured flyer. It advertised a vacation. A long-legged blonde with a hot-pink bikini sat on a strip of white sand and gazed out into a turquoise ocean. There was a faint outline of an island on the horizon.

Lucy felt drawn to the picture. The blonde woman was looking into the distance. Lucy knew that feeling — that's how she had spent the day at school — trying to gaze out, beyond everything. But the woman was sitting someplace called the Bahamas. The words TROPICAL PARADISE jumped off the picture. Lucy sighed, crumpled up the flyer and tossed it out.

Later that evening, Lucy tried experimenting with a new hairstyle. It was an old trick she used to get rid of the blahs. It didn't work this time. Her heart wasn't in it. She called L.D. and talked to her for half an hour, until she could hear L.D.'s dad yell something in the background. They both hung up quickly. Lucy knew nothing else was going to happen. She might as well go to bed.

Sitting in bed, Lucy thought, I could have gone out with Clutch. She had met Clutch through her friend Paul, and was attracted to him. The trouble with Clutch was one minute he was crazy and exciting and the next minute, he could be a jerk. Still, he was one of the most interesting boys around. To begin with, he was older than all of them and he went to Borden High School. When he drove up in his paint-splattered car, everyone clustered around him. Some of the kids called him Mr. Action because he had a reputation for getting bombed at parties.

"Lucy, are you still up?" Her mother's voice drifted up the stairs.

Lucy didn't answer. It was eleven o'clock. Of course she was still up. She could hear her mother climbing the stairs.

"Sorry, honey. Everything got delayed, and then we stopped to get something to eat." Her mother appeared at he bedroom door with her briefcase still tucked under her arm.

"Oh, I know." Lucy carefully examined the hem of her duvet. Her mother held up the briefcase and wrinkled up her face.

"You know, I'm so busy these days, I feel like bailing out. I'd like to head to a deserted island somewhere."

Lucy looked up in surprise. That sounded a lot like the way she felt.

"Where?" she asked.

"Oh, you know — anywhere. I'd just like to have some time out. Everybody needs it sometimes." She came over and gave Lucy a kiss. "It's late now. You'd better turn that light off and get to sleep."

That's it, thought Lucy as she listened to her mother going back downstairs — that has to be the answer. I'm going to bail out of my life for awhile, just the way Mom said. And with that amazing thought she fell instantly asleep.

CHAPTER 2

Lucy woke up the next morning with a jolt. Even though she couldn't remember anything, she knew that she had been dreaming all night. She tried to make herself remember something. Immediately she thought of water. It was pale turquoise-coloured water. Darn, she thought, I'm thinking of that flyer I threw out last night — or was it in my dream? She wasn't sure. It didn't matter because she knew she was ready for today. All she had to do was get to school and tell someone about what she was thinking. L.D. had better be at school.

For once, Lucy didn't stand in front of her closet and worry about what to wear. She grabbed the closest thing she could find and charged down to the kitchen. Her mother was still asleep. There was a note for her next to her place mat on the dining table. Lucy rolled her eyes when she saw it. Probably more arrangements for her because Mom wasn't going to be home. Well, it didn't matter anymore because she had plans of her own. She was almost tempted not to read it, when she noticed that a credit card was placed beside the note. That's a new one, Lucy thought to herself. She picked up the note.

Why don't you invite a friend and book two tickets for the ballet? Just give my Visa number to the booking office. You can do this on the phone.
  Love, Mom.

Lucy knew it was her mother's way of making up for being away so much, but today it didn't matter. She had far more exciting things on her mind than going to the ballet. Even though she took ballet classes, she liked modern jazz a lot more — that's how well her mom knew her. Well, even that didn't hurt so much anymore. Lucy grabbed her lunch, left the note and credit card exactly where she had found them and headed for school.

L.D., Erica and Heather were all gathered

around the lockers when Lucy got to school. Erica was reading everyone's horoscope from the paper. It had become a morning ritual. Erica was convinced that horoscopes were always right. The rest of them just smiled and pretended to look serious. Nobody had the heart to tell Erica that they didn't believe in them.

"How's the boredom factor?" quipped Heather.

"I've handled that, I think I'm going to take off for awhile."

"You'd better read your horoscope first," said Erica.

L.D. just stared at Lucy. Lucy knew they were waiting for her to explain herself. She didn't like the serious look L.D. was giving her. This was the right time to blow everybody's mind.

"I'm taking off for a sunny island," she tossed out airily.

"I know!" shouted Erica triumphantly. "Your parents are taking you away for the March break!"

"Nope."

"Then what?" The twins spoke together.

"I'm heading off by myself, and nobody knows anything about it."

"No way! Come on Lucy, you're just making this up." Heather gave her a puzzled look.

"Wait and see," replied Lucy.

"Lucy! Are you *serious*?" Erica grabbed Lucy's arm.

"Come on, we're going to be late for class," said L.D.

Lucy let the others walk ahead of her. She could hear the twins whispering to each other. L.D. didn't say a word to her, almost as though she hadn't heard what Lucy had said. Lucy smiled to herself. L.D. had heard, all right, she was just going to take her own time in reacting.

L.D. caught up with Lucy at lunch just ahead of the twins.

"You're not serious about what you said this morning," she said bluntly.

"As a matter of fact, I am. I'm sick of everything here, and I'm going to take off."

"You're crazy." L.D. looked confused.

"No, I'm not," announced Lucy. She felt very calm.

"Where are you going to go? What are you up to?" spluttered L.D.

"I'm going to go to one of those islands, you know, like... like the Bahamas!"

"And your parents don't know anything about it, right?"

"Right."

"So what are you going to use for money?"

13

L.D. looked at her curiously.

"Oh, I think I know how to work that out."

"You're crazy," repeated L.D.

Lucy just smiled, and that's when the twins caught up with them.

"C'mon, tell us," begged Heather.

"I've still got lots of planning to do," replied Lucy.

"Can we help? Hey, this is going to be wild!" Erica swung Lucy around.

"Yeah, it is," laughed Lucy. She felt something lighting up inside her.

"Lucy, you've just finished getting over all that trouble you had with Voula," L.D. said indignantly.

Lucy shot her a furious look. Why did L.D. have to bring that up all of a sudden? It was just a phase, as her mother had called it. It had been a wild sort of dare to walk into a store and walk out with something you hadn't paid for. Lucy had apologized, and even paid for it by doing all that community service. Her friend Voula had been with her when she had been caught stealing a sweater. Then Voula's parents decided that Lucy was a bad influence on Voula. The next thing Lucy knew was that Voula had moved away, and the friendship fizzled out. Still, that's how life was. If something awful happened and you got caught, you were in trouble, but eventually it would all pass away. She didn't even miss Voula anymore. How dare L.D. act like such a drip on the day that she was feeling so excited!

"Honestly—" began Lucy.

"Okay, okay, I'm sorry," broke in L.D., seeing the hurt look on Lucy's face.

"Well, I've got to go," announced Lucy.

"You can't go, Lucy, you haven't told us a thing," protested Erica.

"Listen," said Lucy to her, "I don't want you blabbing all over school. Besides, I still have lots of plans to make."

"She may have a mouth, but she's not going to open it this time," said Heather, rescuing her twin.

"Okay," said Lucy slowly, "I'll tell you all about it, but it's got to be kept among ourselves."

"Lucy!" Erica's eyes flashed with indignation. "I won't tell a soul."

After school Lucy and L.D. walked home together. The twins had a meeting for the graduation committee. As she started towards home with L.D., Lucy looked back at Degrassi Junior High. How ugly the old school building looked! A tropical island would never have a place like that. A shiver of excitement rose up her spine. She was about to begin a new adventure, and it was going to be the most daring thing she had ever done. The weekend papers were full of advertisements for trips to the islands. And she'd heard her parents talk about travel agencies. Her father travelled a lot. He was a systems analyst for a computer firm which did business all over the world. Sometimes his plane tickets were even delivered to the house. All she had to do was lock into the system. If you could charge ballet tickets on a credit card, then you could do the same with a vacation.

"I want to know what you're up to." L.D.'s voice broke in on her thoughts.

"L.D., I'm just taking off for awhile."

"How can you go away by yourself?" L.D. gave her a puzzled look.

"Look, missing a week of school is not a big deal."

"It's a big deal when they call the cops and say you're missing."

"Well, that's the part I have to plan. No one is going to know I'm missing," explained Lucy.

"What are you going to do about money and stuff like that?"

"L.D. this is day *one!*" Lucy exploded. "I'm going to work it out. I'd do anything to get away from here for awhile."

16

"Okay, so let's race home and call some travel places," said L.D. moving briskly along the sidewalk.

Lucy looked at L.D. and giggled. That was L.D. — she would put up a big fight, and then come through in a flash — tough as nails one minute, and then a complete pushover the next.

When they got to Lucy's place and headed up to her room, L.D. flung herself on Lucy's bed. Lucy went down and found a bag of cookies and the Yellow Pages telephone book. She ran upstairs with both.

They opened the directory at "Travel Agents". Lucy dialed the first number and asked the person at the other end if they accepted a Visa number on the phone. To her delight, she soon found out that most of them did. Some of them very patiently explained about vacation packages which included meals. Yes, everybody had packages for the Bahamas, and did she have an island in mind? That's when Lucy hung up giggling. It was utterly fantastic. The little, plastic card lying downstairs was the key to the magic kingdom. It was as easy as that.

L.D. took over the phone for awhile, while Lucy scribbled details in her English binder. One agent described a special February offer for a three-night weekend trip. When L.D.

hung up, she looked at Lucy.

"Do you realize that one weekend and a P.D. day could solve the problem?"

"I know," crowed Lucy.

"You could be spending the weekend with one of us."

"I told you I could do it."

"Yeah, but you still have to make sure this card thing works," reminded L.D.

"It has to work," announced Lucy, "— it just has to."

"You have to test it."

"I'm going to. Do you want to go to the ballet this Friday night?"

L.D. paused, "Look, I'd love to, but I can't ask my dad for any money right now. I didn't have a chance to tell you but his garage was broken into a week ago. He doesn't think his insurance is going to cover everything." L.D. turned away to cover her embarrassment.

"It's my mom's treat," broke in Lucy. "You're invited." She touched L.D.'s arm. "I'm sorry about your dad. Don't worry, I'm sure he'll work something out."

"I hope so. Everybody isn't as lucky as you."

"Me? Lucky?" Lucy snorted.

"Yes," said L.D.

"L.D., you don't know everything."

"Maybe not," shrugged L.D. "but you certainly have more than most of the kids we know."

"That's what you think," replied Lucy in a cynical tone.

"Yeah, and I'm right. Are you going to show me how this card works?"

"Watch me," said Lucy.

When she finished ordering the ballet tickets on the telephone by giving her mother's Visa number, L.D. was thoroughly impressed.

CHAPTER 3

"Did you manage to get some tickets for the ballet, Lucy?" asked her mother the next morning.

"No, but I'm going to today, thanks."

Lucy turned away so her mother couldn't see the guilty look that went along with the lie she had just told. She had to hang on to that card until all her plans were made.

"Who did you invite? Let me guess. Could it be L.D., by any chance?"

"You're right."

"Well I'm glad. Poor girl, it must be so difficult for her without a mother." Her mom actually sounded concerned.

"Oh, L.D.'s tough," replied Lucy.

"It's not the same, Lucy," chided her mother. "You should realize how lucky you are to have both your parents."

Lucy looked at her mother in amazement. It was on the tip of her tongue to say, yeah, but L.D.'s dad is home with her a lot more. But she decided all this talk could become dangerous. What if her mother decided to get the tickets herself, and asked for the card back?

"I've got to go, Mom. I have to be in early for some stuff."

"Listen, honey. Daddy called late last night to say his trip has been extended by a few more days. I'm so busy this week I don't even have the time to miss him... how about you?"

"Well, I'm pretty busy too," Lucy said, avoiding the question. Then she picked up her school bag. "I'll see you, Mom."

Lucy let herself out of the front door. She almost wanted to skip along the sidewalk. She was going to L.D.'s place after school and on the way they were going to drop in at a travel agency. Erica had phoned last night to tell them that travel agencies gave out all sorts of free brochures. It was turning out to be great. Her friends were all with her. It would have been awful if she'd had to do everything alone. Sometimes, even when you pretended to be tough and cool, you really needed your friends.

When Lucy got to school, she found Clutch parked in the front. The Clutchmobile seemed to have gotten a little wilder since the last time she had seen it. One of the side doors had a dent on it. The minute Clutch saw her, he jumped out of the car. Lucy quickened her steps. She didn't want to tangle with Clutch this morning.

"Lucy, hey Lucy, wait up," shouted Clutch.

Lucy stopped. She may as well get it over with. She turned around and watched Clutch bouncing up to her. He was such a cool-looking guy. Why was he such a jerk at times?

"Lucy, I've been wanting to talk to you," said Clutch.

"About what?"

"What you said to me."

"I can't remember what I said."

"C'mon Lucy, you said you never wanted to see me again," protested Clutch.

"Oh, yeah. Well, I meant it." Lucy began to turn away.

"Hey, listen. I want to prove something to you. All I want is a chance," Clutch pleaded.

Lucy felt herself softening. Clutch was looking at her intensely. It was difficult to resist that look — maybe there was another side to him. Everything was beginning to turn around in her life right now. She might as well share a bit of it.

"I guess I didn't mean it that way," she said.

"Friends?"

"Friends." Lucy gave Clutch a shy smile.

"Hey!" said Clutch.

"What?"

"You look terrific. Even better than usual." Clutch moved closer to her.

Lucy smiled. "I've got to go, or I'll be late."

"Want a drive home?" offered Clutch.

"Sure," said Lucy, and she walked away.

L.D. was standing outside the front door of Degrassi, watching. She frowned as Lucy came up to her.

"I thought you couldn't stand Clutch."

"He's not that bad, L.D. Besides, everyone deserves a second chance." Lucy felt embarrassed. L.D. could be such a pain sometimes.

"I hope you're not going to encourage him."

"All he's going to do is give us a drive home."

"That's if he doesn't get drunk somewhere in between," snorted L.D.

But L.D. was wrong. Clutch turned up after school, the car radio blaring and not a trace of anything suspicious on his breath. When he saw L.D. with Lucy, he didn't bat an eyelid. He just hopped out and opened the back door for L.D.

Lucy jumped into the front seat and a mouthed a silent "I told you" to L.D.

"So, where do we drop you, L.D.?" Clutch turned around and grinned at L.D.

"Actually, you drop both of us at this travel agency," Lucy said.

"Both!" squawked Clutch.

"Yeah, we have a date," sniggered L.D.

"Oh, I see," muttered Clutch, giving Lucy a disappointed look. Lucy turned around and shot a furious look at L.D. Here was Clutch trying hard to be nice, and L.D. was making fun of him.

Clutch turned his radio a little higher, and L.D. jumped when the rear speaker blasted her ear off. She glared at Clutch. Clutch kept his eyes on the road.

"So, who's going on a trip?" he asked.

Both Lucy and L.D. kept quiet. L.D. gave Lucy a warning nudge from behind.

"I've got to pick up some stuff for my mom," replied Lucy.

"It's just two blocks down on Queen," L.D. said pointedly.

"If you just have to pick up stuff, I can wait," said Clutch hopefully.

"No, it may take awhile. Thanks anyway," said Lucy.

She was starting to feel bad about using Clutch like this. When they got to the travel agency, she thanked him warmly.

"Do you want to go out tonight?" he asked.

"Sorry, I can't," said Lucy. "L.D. and I have to work on this project... but I'll call you," she added quickly.

"Don't forget," said Clutch. He gave Lucy another intense look.

"I won't," she promised.

"Lucy," L.D. warned, "he's going to be all over you again."

Lucy just shrugged, but inside she was smiling. She waved to him and he honked the horn twice as he shot away from the curb. L.D. rolled her eyes in disgust.

The travel agency had racks of brochures right at the entrance. Further down there were two desks where two young women sat with phones plastered to their ears. One of them lifted a hand and gave a friendly wave to Lucy and L.D. Neither one of them knew what to do. They decided that the safest thing was to look at the brochures. The scenes of islands and sparkling oceans swirled before them. It was almost as good as looking at the ice cream bins at Baskin-Robbins. There was so much variety. All the people in the pictures looked tanned and happy. Lucy bit her lip in excitement, and L.D.'s eyes widened.

"Bliss city," whispered Lucy.

"Oh, *wow*." L.D. was impressed.

"Can I help you girls?" said a voice.

One of the travel agents had put her phone down and was giving them a wide, friendly smile.

"C'mon, let's ask her," whispered L.D. dragging Lucy with her.

"Thinking of a vacation?" said the travel agent.

Lucy perched on the edge of the chair in front of the desk.

"I'm thinking of going to the Bahamas," she said smoothly. "I guess you must have a package for it?"

"Yes, lots. Do you have your dates?"

"Er... not yet, but I will soon."

"Well, there are packages for a week, two weeks, and even some for the three-night special," rattled off the travel agent.

"Terrific," said Lucy.

"Are you lucky kids being treated by your parents?"

"Yeah, something like that," mumbled Lucy.

"March break, eh?"

"It could be earlier. Can we just get some information on the Bahamas?" Lucy's pulse was racing.

"I think you girls would have a blast in Nassau. Of course there are also the out islands," explained the travel agent. She went over to the racks of brochures and selected several.

"Why don't I give you my card, and when you have your dates, just call. Here are some packages to the Bahamas — great deals," she said.

Her phone rang and while she answered it, she gave Lucy another stack of pamphlets and her card.

Lucy put everything into her school bag and walked out with L.D. Now all they had to do was go over to L.D.'s place and choose one of the vacation packages. She had to make that decision tonight because her mom would ask for her card back.

CHAPTER 4

L.D.'s house was quite close to Queen Street. Whenever Lucy went over there she felt the contrast between their two streets. L.D.'s street was rather peculiar. It started with a few shops which abruptly straggled to a halt, and then a row of small, unrenovated houses bunched up ahead. Her father's garage was next to the last house. Lucy knew the garage from the outside but had never been inside.

As they approached it, L.D. said, "I have to pop in just to tell him I'm home."

"You mean you have to clock in?" asked Lucy.

"Well, he's been pretty jumpy since the break-in.... I guess he worries about me," replied L.D.

Lucy followed L.D. up to the garage,

wondering why she had never felt that her father worried about her. When L.D. marched up to the shabby-looking door Lucy noticed that the window beside it was covered with plywood. Bits of jagged glass stuck out of the frame. L.D. caught her glance. "Yeah, that's how they got in," she said sourly.

Entering the garage was another shock. They walked into a gloomy, little room entirely filled up with a rough, dusty table littered with paper.

"This is the office," said L.D. She walked behind the desk to push open another door.

"Oh..." said Lucy, wondering how anybody could call the grubby, little room an office.

"Come on. He's in the back — in the shop," muttered L.D. gesturing over her shoulder.

The large, concrete room was filled up by two cars. One of them had the hood open, and the other was slightly raised on a hoist.

L.D. walked up to the raised car and yelled, "Hi Dad!"

"L.D.?" asked a muffled voice from underneath the car.

Lucy moved closer to L.D. She jumped when a pair of shoes followed by legs slid out from underneath the car. L.D. shot her a mischievous look.

"Come to see your old dad," said Mr.

Delacorte wiping his grease-covered hands on his trousers.

"We're just going home."

"Hi, Lucy," said Mr.Delacorte giving her a friendly smile.

"Hi," said Lucy not able to tear her gaze from Mr. Delacorte's large hands where a crescent of black dirt rimmed each fingernail.

"Bet your father doesn't get his hands looking like this," chuckled Mr. Delacorte.

Lucy grinned weakly in embarrassment. She looked nervously at L.D., but L.D. was giving her dad a steadfast, affectionate look. She's not embarrassed, thought Lucy. She's right there with him, pleased and even proud.

"When are you going to get the window fixed, Dad?" asked L.D.

"I have to collect the glass tomorrow," replied Mr.Delacorte.

A small frown appeared on his face.

"What if they come back?" asked L.D. She looked worried.

"I have some bars I'm going to put up. Besides, they can't take anything else."

Lucy noticed the weary shrug Mr. Delacorte gave. She didn't know what to say. It was strange watching L.D. have this conversation with her dad. She sounded so grown-up and involved with her dad's work. I don't even know what my father really does at his office, thought Lucy. At that moment she felt envious of L.D.

"Do you girls want a Coke?" asked Mr. Delacorte.

"No, thanks," murmured Lucy.

"We'll get something at the house. I know you need to get under that car again." L.D. reached over and gave her father a quick kiss on the cheek.

"Bye, honey. Good to see you again, Lucy. L.D., I want you to make sure that you lock the front door."

"Okay," L.D. replied.

"Bye, Mr. Delacorte," Lucy added.

When they were outside, L.D. rolled her eyes. "He's still a little nervous."

"I'm sorry it happened to your dad," said Lucy.

"Oh he'll handle it, he's a pretty terrific person," said L.D.

"I wish my father was like that," muttered Lucy.

"What do you mean?" L.D. had a startled look on her face.

"Nothing...."

"Nothing?" repeated L.D.

"*Nothing*," said Lucy curtly, walking a little faster than L.D.

When L.D. opened the door to the house, they could hear the telephone ringing. It was Erica, wanting to know if she and Heather could come over. They didn't want to miss a minute of the great caper. Why not, thought Lucy — the more the merrier. L.D. decided that if they were having company, she may as well produce some snacks.

Lucy watched L.D. open the fridge and sigh.

"Not too many goodies around," said L.D.

"Who cares? I'm not hungry."

"Do you think they eat popcorn?" asked L.D.

"Isn't that a lot of work?" said Lucy, hating the pinched look on L.D.'s face.

"Well, I have to have something," muttered L.D.

Lucy knew that L.D. was embarrassed because she couldn't find any fancy snacks in her kitchen. Looking at the sparsely equipped kitchen and the tiny house, you could tell there wasn't much money around.

"We were supposed to go shopping on the weekend," said L.D. apologetically, "but then we had the break-in...."

"It's okay," said Lucy.

"I just don't want to bother him about extra things these days."

"Come on, let's make popcorn," said Lucy.

She wanted to change the subject.

Lucy watched L.D. pour a little bit of oil in a large pot and toss in a cup of kernels. She was amazed. Her mother had this electrical popcorn maker with a fancy lid, and here L.D. was just using a regular cooking pot.

"Now, hang on for the great part," whispered L.D., as she put the lid on.

The corn started popping in sharp explosions. Lucy jumped at the first sound and L.D. burst out laughing. The doorbell rang. It was the twins. They sailed in with their curls flying and eyes sparkling.

"Have you done it?" asked Erica, flinging herself down on a kitchen chair.

"Wheels said he saw you driving off with Clutch." Heather's eyes were filled with curiosity.

"Yeah, he gave us a ride to the travel agency," Lucy explained.

"Some ride!" snorted L.D. "He almost destroyed my right ear with his radio."

"*L.D.*," protested Lucy.

Luckily Erica jumped in again. She wanted to know what was happening with the plans. Lucy pulled out the travel brochures and they studied them while they munched on popcorn. Lucy knew it was going to be easier to get away for three nights than a whole week. Besides, it didn't cost so much.

She had heard her mom sometimes complain about her charge card bills, but money had never been a problem in her family. Her allowance was larger than her friends'. "You're our only child, Lucy — we want you to have the best in life," her mother had always said. She didn't even have to do any household chores. All she had to do was put up with absent parents.

"Look at this." L.D. shoved a pink paper under Lucy's nose.

SUPER-SAVER SPECIAL — THREE NIGHTS FOR $299 read the heading on the page. The trip was from Friday afternoon to Monday afternoon, and the dates were next week! Lucy gazed at the page, mesmerized. It was perfect. Somebody had arranged this trip just for her. All she had to do was to pick up the telephone and book it. It was as simple as that.

"Let me see." Heather tried to peer over Lucy's shoulder.

"That's the one," said Lucy, giving the paper to her.

"You'd have to cut half a day of school," said L.D.

"Say you're spending the weekend with us," Erica offered.

"You could tell them Monday was a P.D.

day, so you get home Monday night."

"They're going to call your mom if you don't turn up at school on Monday," warned L.D.

"Well, I'm just going to have to make sure that doesn't happen," replied Lucy.

"I know... you can take a note in on Friday saying that you won't be in school on Monday," tossed out Erica.

"It'd better be a *very* convincing letter," mumbled Heather.

"Don't worry, I've done it before," said Lucy.

"You've done a lot of things before that you've regretted." L.D. shot Lucy a meaningful look.

"What's that supposed to mean?" Lucy was furious.

"You know what I mean," said L.D. quietly. "I guess I'm just a worrier."

"Well, don't worry, I can take care of it all," Lucy snapped at L.D.

"So I guess that's taken care of." L.D. just shrugged her shoulders.

It was all falling into place. Lucy closed her eyes, and the image of a turquoise ocean swam before her. If she tried hard enough, she could hear palm trees rustling in the breeze. It was a totally mind-blowing sensation. She was going to leave everything behind and escape to a tropical paradise, just the way the brochures described it.

"Are you going to do it?" asked L.D.

"Yes," said Lucy. She reached into her wallet for her mother's credit card.

"Wait a minute," said Erica.

"What?"

"You better use a grown-up voice."

"I'll manage. " Lucy tried to sound confident.

"Everybody keep quiet," said L.D., turning her ghetto-blaster off. "We don't want them to think we're a bunch of crazy kids."

"Good idea," said Heather. She clapped a hand over Erica's mouth.

Lucy took a deep breath, walked to the phone on the kitchen wall and dialed the number. The call took about three minutes. The travel agent on the other end didn't seem to have any problem with Lucy's voice. All she wanted was the card number and expiry date. Did Lucy want to have the ticket mailed to her?

"No," said Lucy. "Can I pick it up at the airport?"

"Certainly," said the travel agent, "may we have a contact telephone number for you?" Lucy gave her L.D.'s number.

She hung up the phone with shaky fingers. Something strange was happening inside her. It was a feeling she hadn't felt for a long time — not since she had stolen the sweater. It was a sick kind of excitement, the sort of excitement that had a dark shadow around it. The shadow hung around until you switched off your mind. Well, she'd better switch off her mind now. She wasn't going to let anything spoil her plans.

"What did she say? What did she say?" shrieked Erica.

"It's all done."

"Oh, boy! Lucy, you are *so* cool," exclaimed Heather.

"I'm off, I'm off next Friday." Lucy clasped her legs and rocked back and forth.

"I'll believe it on Friday," said L.D. slowly.

Since the excitement was over, the twins took off. Lucy and L.D. sat and talked about the trip for awhile. They still had some more plans to make. Neither one of them knew how to get to the airport. They had to find out about that, and plan what Lucy had to take with her. Before they knew it, it was almost 6:30. Lucy picked up her school bag and threw all the travel brochures except the pink one in the garbage.

"Bye, L.D.," said Lucy.

"What time does the ballet start tomorrow?"

"Eight. Come over at seven. My mom's

37

even given me cab fare."

"Ritzy," drawled L.D. She gave Lucy a wicked grin.

When Lucy got home, her phone was ringing. It was her mother. She told Lucy that she'd be home in an hour. Lucy hung up and opened the fridge to see the supper her mom had prepared. But she wasn't hungry. All that popcorn at L.D.'s place had filled her up. And the old, sick, excited feeling was coming back, now that she was alone. She decided to call Clutch. He answered his phone on the first ring, almost as though he was waiting for her call.

"Is L.D. with you?" he asked.

"No."

"Just checking, thought maybe you both were inseparable, or something."

Lucy giggled. Clutch started chuckling as well. Lucy was tempted to tell Clutch everything. But it was too early to start trusting him so much — maybe she'd tell him next week.

"Do you want to go to a movie tomorrow night?" he asked.

"I'm sorry, I'm going to the ballet."

"The ballet! Do you like that kind of stuff?"

"No... not really... but I'm kind of stuck," Lucy tried to explain.

"I guess you're going with your parents."

"No, I'm going with L.D." The moment she said it, Lucy wished she hadn't.

"See, I was right, you are inseparable," said Clutch. He sounded disgusted. "Can't you stand her up or something?"

"I'm sorry, Clutch. It's been arranged for awhile."

Do I sound like a snob, wondered Lucy. The phone call was beginning to feel like a mistake.

"Okay, okay. How about Saturday?" asked Clutch.

"Sure," said Lucy quickly.

"Should I call you, or is it a date?"

"I guess it's a date."

"By the way..." added Clutch.

"What?"

"L.D.'s not invited."

Lucy started giggling as she hung up.

Lucy was rummaging around in a pile of summer clothes when her mom came home. Lucy quickly shoved the pile under her bed and ran downstairs to greet her.

"You haven't eaten anything." Her mother was standing in front of the open fridge.

"I stuffed myself on popcorn at L.D.'s place," Lucy explained.

"Well, come and sit with me," said her

mom, zapping some cannelloni in the microwave.

Lucy found it difficult to sit with her mom and have a normal conversation. She kept expecting her to ask for her credit card. But her mother chattered about all sorts of things.

"When your dad gets back, maybe we can all go out to dinner together." Her mom jabbed at the cannelloni on her plate half-heartedly.

"Yeah," replied Lucy coldly.

"Don't you want to, Lucy?"

Lucy fought the small tide of irritation rising within her and looked at her mother. "Both of you are so busy, nothing we plan together seems to work out anymore."

"That's not fair, Lucy. That's a ridiculous thing to say," said her mother.

"I'm sorry," broke in Lucy.

"Well, I am too... both of us have very demanding jobs, but it doesn't mean we're abandoning you," cried her mother indignantly.

Lucy kept quiet. She didn't want to get into anything really heavy with her mother tonight. She had other things on her mind.

An uncomfortable silence hung around the kitchen table and Lucy avoided the reproachful look in her mother's eyes. She plonked a piece of cannelloni on her plate just to please her. After she had pushed it around with her fork for awhile, she knew it was time to escape to her room.

"I'm going to bed." Lucy stood up.

Her mother just nodded at her silently. Lucy hurriedly rinsed her plate in the sink and stuck it in the dishwasher. She ran upstairs and locked her bedroom door. Then she pulled out the pile of summer clothes she had shoved under the bed. Her old, black, high-cut bathing suit was still there. Lucy wiggled out of her clothes, and pulled it on. It seemed to fit all right, but she didn't have a full-length mirror in her room. She opened her door quietly and started to tiptoe to her parents' bedroom. She was half-way down the hall when she saw her mother coming up.

"Lucy!" Her mother look startled. "What's going on?"

Lucy folded her arms protectively around her. "I just wanted to see if it still fit."

"In the middle of winter?"

"Somebody wanted to borrow it. She's the same size... but I thought I'd just make sure," mumbled Lucy.

"Lucy, you don't lend your bathing suit," said her mother. "It's very personal."

"Yeah, well, I said I'd just look... that's all," stammered Lucy, edging towards her door.

Lucy entered her room and shut the door. As she leaned against it with her face flushed and burning, a chill went through her body. Had she fooled her mother? There was no sound in the hall but she felt her mother's eyes boring through her closed door. Lucy opened the door silently, just a crack. The hall was empty and her mother's bedroom door was shut. Lucy hastily shut her door, peeled off the bathing suit and tossed it under her bed.

CHAPTER 5

Lucy overslept the next morning. She remembered her mother walking in and telling her to get up, but she'd fallen asleep again. Last night it had taken her a long time to go to sleep. Now it seemed that she had only been asleep for a moment, and it was time to get up. What a drag! When she realized that she was going to be late, she was almost tempted to stay in bed.

There was another problem. She had not done her Math homework. It was due today. The worst thing in the world was being chewed out by a teacher in front of the whole class. This day was going to be a grind. Maybe she should pretend she had the flu or something. But the thought of staying home alone all day didn't appeal to her either, so she dragged herself up. While she was brushing her teeth, she noticed that she had circles under her eyes. She was going to go school looking like an absolute wreck — that bothered her. The look was so important — most of the time it was just as important as grades.

Getting a late slip from Doris, the school secretary, was another pain. By the time she walked into her first class there were only ten minutes left in the period. Everybody looked at her and grinned.

"Where were you?" whispered L.D.

"Fast asleep."

Between classes, Lucy went to the washroom. The circles under her eyes were beginning to fade. She pulled out her eyeliner and drew a line under her eyes. Now she was beginning to look like herself. Some of the younger girls were standing in front of the mirrors applying make-up. Lucy looked at them and smiled. She knew they were doing it at school because their parents disapproved. She had never had that hassle. She could walk out of her house wearing whatever she wanted.

Lucy spent the rest of the day daydreaming through her classes. Six more days, and she was going to be sitting on a plane. She was going to have the biggest adventure in her life. There were still a few loose ends to tie up, but L.D. had promised to help, and it was all going to work out.

After last period, Lucy went to her locker to collect her bag. She found Erica poring over a fashion magazine.

"Lucy, look." She held up the magazine. "Have you ever seen such gorgeous bathing suits?"

Lucy looked at the page. They were gorgeous all right. The caption said "Cruise Wear". The three models were lying on a beach wearing the most amazing bikinis. Sizzling scraps of vibrant lycra were arranged over their tanned and glistening bodies.

"You have the long legs for this," said Erica, jabbing her finger at the page.

Lucy looked at the bathing suits. She knew she could die for one of them, and Erica was right, she had the figure for them. She was going to have to do something about it. She just had to get a bikini to take along with her. Lucy looked at the bottom of the page to see where they were sold, but it was an American magazine and the stores listed underneath were somewhere in New York.

She handed the magazine back to Erica and turned to her locker. Pulling her things out, she slammed it shut and raced out. L.D. was waiting for her at the front door.

"I've seen the most fantastic thing," Lucy said enthusiastically.

"What is it?"

"L.D., do you think I'd look good in a bikini?"

L.D. looked at her as if she were crazy and folded her arms across her chest, waiting for an explanation.

"Erica had this fashion magazine. It had some great bathing suits in it. I need something like that for my trip," Lucy announced.

"Yeah, and a mink coat." L.D. didn't look convinced.

"I'm serious," said Lucy. She followed L.D. down the school steps.

"Well, Lucy, I'm not really into clothes the way you are."

"I *am*," said Lucy fiercely. "I can't take that grungy, black suit with me."

"I hope you're not —"

"No, I'm not," Lucy reassured her. Didn't L.D. know she was through with the shoplifting for good?

"On the subject of clothes, what are we supposed to wear tonight?" asked L.D.

"Whatever you like," replied Lucy, knowing that L.D. didn't have a lot of fancy outfits.

"Thanks a lot... I guess I'll find something... I'll be over after dinner."

Lucy raced home. Her mom wasn't there, so she could get out the pile of summer clothes hiding under her bed and choose stuff for her trip. The ballet performance didn't start till eight, and she'd have plenty of time. She also wanted to call the travel agency and check on her trip once again — just to be sure. The travel agent confirmed that her trip was booked. She had to be at the airport two hours before the flight took off.

Lucy grabbed a bag of chips from the kitchen and headed up to her room. Her summer clothes were a big jumble. She had walking shorts and denim cut-offs, lots of little tank tops and even a long flowing Indian muslin skirt. The only eyesore was her one-piece bathing suit. After she had seen the bikinis, it just didn't look right anymore.

Her mother was very good about giving her money to buy clothes, but it was going to be hard to explain that she wanted to buy a bikini in the middle of winter. She was going to have to think of an excuse. Tomorrow morning, she was going to hit the stores — maybe go to the Eaton Centre. It had millions of clothing stores. She could spend the whole day looking for a bikini, and then go with Clutch to the movies in the evening.

She also needed a suitcase. She went down

to the basement, where her parents stashed everything like that. But the suitcases that she found were all large. Her dad had taken the smaller one. The only thing a little smaller was her duffle bag from camp. It was plastered with stickers and funny messages. I'm just going for three days, Lucy told herself, it'll be ideal.

That's when Lucy thought of her mother, and how well-dressed she always looked. Even when she travelled, she looked neat. How was Lucy going to look in the hotel of the Tropical Paradise when she checked in with her camp duffle bag? Maybe the twins had a more respectable-looking suitcase. Appearances — they were beginning to become a trap. Part of Lucy hated this trap. It seemed to rule so much of her life. This was the Lucy she had built up, so carefully, almost layer by layer. Somewhere, deep inside, had to be another Lucy. Or was she just kidding herself? Why did the appearance never quite match up to what she felt inside? She wanted to be free, or was it carefree? With some of these confusing thoughts churning inside her, Lucy reluctantly marched up with the duffle bag.

When L.D. arrived at seven, she was wearing her going-out uniform. She definitely needed some make-up and earrings, thought

Lucy.

"I have a great scarf to go with your sweater," she said dragging L.D. up to her room.

"Lucy, I really don't want to put on anything... that's too much," protested L.D. weakly.

"Come on L.D.," said Lucy firmly, "don't you want to at least look your age?"

Half an hour later Lucy and L.D. walked into the O'Keefe Centre. The foyer was packed with enthusiastic people who had come to see the visiting Russian ballet troupe. Lucy and L.D. pushed their way through the clusters of people to the ticket window. It was very simple. The tickets were just waiting for them in a little, white envelope. There was no signing or even showing her mother's Visa card.

The ballet performance was spectacular. There was a male dancer who looked like Clutch and the sets were breathtaking. Lucy discovered that she enjoyed every minute of it.

When she got home her mother was waiting. "Did you and L.D. have a good time?" asked her mother.

"Yeah, it was terrific."

"Do you remember going to see *The Nutcracker* with me when you were younger?"

"I don't think so."

"Well, we did," said her mother. "You were about nine."

"I guess that was a long time ago," said Lucy. She gave her mother a cool look, and had the satisfaction of seeing her look away.

At that instant Lucy knew that if her mom didn't mind spending sixty dollars on the ballet tickets, then she wouldn't make a fuss about another three hundred dollars.

"Guess what? I've been invited for a weekend sleep-over at the twins'," said Lucy.

"When?"

"Next weekend, and there's also a birthday party."

"Oh what fun," exclaimed her mother, "I suppose you need to get a present."

"Two presents. They're twins remember." said Lucy smoothly.

Somehow after the first lie, all the other lies just tumbled out. Lucy felt as though she had no control over what she was saying, but it was working. Her mom didn't have a clue about what was going on, and that was exactly the way Lucy wanted to keep it.

CHAPTER 6

Lucy woke up the next morning and bounced out of bed. This was going to be a wonderful day. She was going to look for a bikini. Her mom had even offered to drive her to the Eaton Centre. Lucy said she was meeting L.D. there. It was another lie — she wasn't. Lucy just didn't want her mom trailing along while she looked for a bikini.

It was Saturday morning and her mom was in the kitchen with all sorts of pans spread on the kitchen counter.

"How would you like eggs benedict?"

"Sure," replied Lucy.

"Your dad used to make them for me, when we first got married," said her mom.

Lucy knew her mom was feeling stressed about how busy they both had become. Why did they live such crazy lives, she thought.

They seemed to be away from each other, and from her most of the time. When her dad got home he would have some kind of glamourous gift for each of them. It really did not make up for all that they seemed to be missing. I'm not going to be like them when I grow up, Lucy vowed to herself silently.

The other awful part was that they didn't even have any family in Toronto. All their relatives lived in New York. L.D. had all these aunts and cousins. The twins had a really groovy grandmother who played bingo, and when she won the jackpot she would take the twins to a bookstore called Britnell's and get them to buy classic novels — no swoony, hot, romance paperbacks, but real books. Even though the twins complained about the books, she knew they adored their grandmother. The last time Lucy had seen her grandparents was three years ago. They lived in Florida in a boxy, little apartment, and didn't want to travel anymore. So getting to see them meant going on a family vacation, but her parents had been much too busy to do that lately.

"Well, here you are," said her mom, serving her a plateful of fancy eggs with a runny sauce all over them.

Lucy was too excited to feel hungry, but she ate the eggs anyway. Actually, they weren't bad. It was like having supper first thing in the morning. Her mom was a pretty fancy cook when she was around.

After breakfast, they hopped into the car and her mom dropped her outside the Eaton Centre.

"Lucy." Her mom had a nervous look on her face.

"Yes," said Lucy, opening the car door.

"Honey, please be careful. Don't get into any trouble."

Lucy looked at her mother resentfully. It seemed that her mom still thought about the shoplifting. It was all over, hadn't she proved that to her?

"Don't worry, Mom," she said, gritting her teeth.

"I don't," said her mom quickly — too quickly.

Saturday shoppers were packed into the Eaton Centre. All the stores had shop windows exploding with colour. Some of the little boutiques had racks of bathing suits. As she looked through one rack, a salesgirl approached her. Her hair was dyed red and had little silvery-black streaks running through it. She wore hanging bunches of crystals as earrings and at least five little diamond studs up one ear lobe. Her tiny miniskirt and jacket looked as though they were made of rubber, and the black spike heels she wore seemed to be at least five inches long.

"Let me show you something sensational," she cooed at Lucy. She drew out a lavender and silver bikini.

"This one is perfect for you." She gave Lucy a brilliant smile.

Lucy looked at the wispy bikini dangling on the plastic hanger. It looked pretty spectacular.

"Come on, let's try it on." The salesgirl was walking towards one of the dressing cubicles.

Lucy went into the dressing room and shut the door. The salesgirl stood outside. It was a wild bikini all right. It made Lucy feel as though she had nothing on. She looked sort of like the models in the travel brochures. Her legs seemed longer than she remembered. The skimpy bikini top made her look as though she had a fuller chest. Erica had been right when she had shown that fashion magazine to her. She could wear a bikini. If only she didn't feel so bare!

"Can I see?" the salesgirl called from outside.

Suddenly Lucy felt shy. But the salesgirl had already opened the door.

"*Knockout!*" She widened her eyes.

"I'm not quite sure," said Lucy. The

thought of wearing the bikini in public was making her nervous.

"Not sure!" The salesgirl looked appalled. "You're going to blow everybody away!"

That was something Lucy could relate to. She liked to do that at school — put together something crazy and have all the girls at Degrassi talking about it.

"Are you going south?"

"Yeah, to a tropical paradise," Lucy giggled.

"Listen, every guy on the beach is going to die," the salesgirl said firmly.

"You think so?" asked Lucy.

"Trust me, just trust me." The salesgirl backed out of the dressing room. "Hang on. I have a great wrap-skirt that goes with it."

Ten minutes later Lucy was standing outside the store with a tiny plastic bag. Inside the bag lay the lavender and silver suit. She had wanted to buy the wrap-skirt too, but she didn't have enough money. This was the first time Lucy had let somebody else convince her to buy something. There was something so sophisticated about the salesgirl, and she had admired Lucy's figure. Lucy felt she had almost looked envious. It was a heady sensation.

Lucy dug out a quarter and headed for a phone. She called L.D.

"You won't believe what I just bought."

"A new outfit, you spoiled brat."

"L.D., I've just bought this sensational bikini," whispered Lucy over the phone.

"What's it like?"

"It's pretty small, but it looks terrific."

"I want to see it... when are you going to be home?"

"L.D. I'm supposed to be with you so you can't just show up there now." Lucy stumbled over the explanation.

"You are?"

"Yeah, well I had to tell her something."

"I don't know how you can lie to your mother about everything," came L.D.'s reproach.

"What do you mean?"

"Nothing... I just don't think I could do it — that's all."

"Do you want to give me a lecture about this?" demanded Lucy, really hating L.D. at that moment.

"No... I guess not," replied L.D. in a reluctant sort of way.

"Thanks a lot," said Lucy sarcastically.

"So why don't you come over tonight?" suggested L.D.

"I can't, I'm going to see a movie with Clutch."

Lucy could almost hear wheels turning in

L.D.'s brain. After awhile, L.D. said, "Okay, I'll talk to you tomorrow."

Lucy hung around at the Eaton Centre for awhile. She had shopped in twenty minutes, and she wasn't quite ready to go home. She poked around some of the other stores, and found out that when you weren't buying you could get hassled at the stores by the staff.

When she left after an hour, she took the bus home. She wanted to try the bikini on again. Her mom wasn't home. Lucy walked to her mom's bedroom and shut the door. She peeled off her clothes, and tried on the bathing suit. It looked just as good as it had at the store. It didn't even feel quite that bare anymore, Lucy decided — you could get used to anything, if you did it more than once.

She took off the bikini and slipped it in the duffle bag under her bed. She was dying to call Erica and tell her about it. The twins were out when she tried telephoning them. Lucy poked around at her mother's dressing table for a while trying on make-up and her jewelry, until she heard her mother return.

"How was the shopping trip, Lucy?" asked her mother.

"Oh great, just great."

"Can I see what you got?"

"Oh—" Lucy jumped, startled.

"So what did you get?" her mother asked.

"Oh... L.D. took it... she has this great idea for wrapping it," Lucy stuttered.

"Well... what was it?"

"We got them matching bikinis, lavender and silver bikinis," said Lucy very slowly.

"Oh, you girls," laughed her mom, totally surprising her.

"I'm going to get something to drink," said Lucy turning away from her mother.

Lucy walked down to the kitchen. She felt a little breathless, and her palms felt sweaty. She'd never done such fast thinking before. It made her think of what L.D. had said about lying. What was happening to L.D., anyway? One minute she was right there being a friend, and the next minute she would get really snippy. She wasn't being herself, not since the break-in at her dad's garage. Or was she just jealous? The infuriating part was that her comment did give Lucy some pangs of guilt, but what L.D. didn't know was that Lucy couldn't stop herself — one quick story after another, and the sick feeling that she would get caught — but her mother was so preoccupied with her own life, she would believe almost anything. Well, for the time being that suited Lucy just fine.

Later that the evening when Clutch pulled up outside her house, Lucy was a little nervous. She didn't want her mom to see the

Clutchmobile parked outside their house. She hadn't really told her mother too much about Clutch. Her friends from Degrassi were okay, but somebody who was almost eighteen and from Borden High could be a bit much even for her parents. Also she had the feeling that somehow her mom wouldn't like Clutch.

Lucy ran upstairs to her mother's room, stuck her head in and asked "Are you going to be home tonight?"

"Lucy, I have to take some clients out for awhile, but I won't be late."

"Oh, that's okay, I'm going to the movies."

"I hope it's a neighbourhood theatre."

"I don't know, Mom. We haven't decided."

"Do you need a ride?" asked her mother.

"I'm going to meet the gang at the corner."

"Maybe we can send out for some Chinese food later tonight."

"Sure... bye Mom."

Lucy raced downstairs and walked out of the house. Clutch grinned from the car.

"What are we going to see?" asked Lucy as she slid into the car.

"How about the Eddie Murphy film?"

Lucy smiled at Clutch. "Sure," she said, "that'd be terrific."

CHAPTER 7

It was not a typical day at Degrassi. While Lucy was being submitted to an unpleasant lecture by Mr. Garcia for having failed the last Math test, her friends were having a conversation which would have devastated her.

"You know, L.D.," said Heather, lacing up her sneakers for their Monday afternoon Gym class, "Erica and I have been discussing Lucy all weekend."

L.D. pulled on her gym shorts and sat next to Heather. They had two minutes to get to Gym, but Heather had a strange expression on her face.

"We don't think what she's doing is quite right," continued Heather.

"What are you trying to say?" asked L.D.

"It's almost as bad as shoplifting."

"You're a great friend," snorted L.D.

"That's not fair," protested Heather.

"You and Erica were the ones who got excited."

Heather didn't reply. L.D. was right, they had all been so excited, just swept up with Lucy's plans. They all wanted to fly off to a sunny island in the middle of this wretched February, and Lucy was the one who was going to do it — maybe do it for all of them, but they were also encouraging her to do something that was not right.

"We're going to be late," said L.D. getting up and flashing Heather a cool look.

"L.D. let's meet after school, please.... I really need to talk to you about this."

"I'll see you at the steps," L.D. tossed over her shoulder, and walked away.

When last period was over, L.D. went off to find the twins. They were waiting for her near the front steps.

"Not here," said L.D. moving towards the back of the school, "I don't want Lucy to bump into us."

The twins had uneasy expressions on their faces. L.D. could be quite ferocious if she wanted to.

"Okay Heather, what do you want to do about this?"

"I guess we're feeling a little scared,"

jumped in Erica, instinctively protecting her twin.

"What if she gets caught, we all get caught," blurted Heather.

"Look, Lucy's got everything planned... and we promised to help." L.D. didn't look ferocious, she just looked bewildered.

"Well, we're not backing out or anything... but we just feel that it's not right."

"You sound like you've already backed out," cried L.D.

"L.D., Lucy may not be stealing from a store but she's stealing from her parents." Heather's face was flushed.

"They won't mind, they spend tons of money on her anyway," replied L.D.

"Yeah, so she could ask... couldn't she," said Erica.

"I don't believe this," muttered L.D. giving both of them a disgusted look.

"We really don't know what to do," said Heather looking miserable.

"I'll tell you what to do," announced L.D., finally looking quite fierce. "I've had some problems with this too, but I know that you never let your friends down, once you've given them your word."

"We don't want to let Lucy down," said the twins, quickly.

"She's supposed to be spending the

weekend at your place, *remember?*"

"Yeah, and we'll do it, but we thought maybe we could talk..." said Heather.

"There's nothing else to say. If you're backing out, tell me right now because Lucy's depending on you," L.D. reminded them.

"We're not backing out, and don't you dare say anything to Lucy about this," said Erica in a low voice.

"About what?" asked a voice behind them.

All three of them jumped. It was Lucy who had just appeared.

"I've been looking everywhere for you, what's going on?"

Erica and Heather had guilty expressions on their faces and L.D. looked mad. I bet they're talking about Clutch, Lucy thought. None of them were very keen on her seeing him. Besides they had such guilty expressions, she was probably right.

"Talking about Clutch?" asked Lucy giving them a broad smile.

"Sort of," mumbled L.D. in relief.

"We've got to go," said the twins, grateful to escape.

"Erica, wait till I show you what I got on Saturday," yelled Lucy after them.

"Okay, call us later," shouted back Erica.

L.D. walked along with Lucy, half-listening to her. She was lost in her own world. It

wasn't just the twins who were beginning to
have second thoughts, but she couldn't admit
that to them. Lucy was her best friend and
she would die before she let her down. So
here she was trapped in the middle of her
own thoughts. All she knew was that somehow her friendship was being tested. Lucy
would be horrified if she found out.

"You haven't heard a word of what I've
said," came Lucy's voice from her side.

"Yes I have," replied L.D.

"So what do you think?"

"It'll be fine," nodded L.D., pretending to
agree with whatever Lucy had been saying.

"I'm going to do it tonight," announced
Lucy.

"Why tonight?" asked L.D., wondering
what it was that Lucy was going to do.

"Because there're just three days left."

"How could I forget!"

"Besides, I think I can trust him. Do you
want to come as well?" Lucy looked at L.D.
hesitantly.

"Where?" said L.D. giving up.

"To the airport dummy. Clutch'll drive us,"
said Lucy with her eyes sparkling and her
cheeks flushed with excitement.

L.D. rolled her eyes — so that was what
she had missed. Lucy was going to ask
Clutch to drive her to the airport. She

couldn't picture his wreck of a car ever making it to the airport — still, it was the only arrangement in sight. She wasn't going to tell Lucy but she would find out if there were any buses that went to the airport — just in case....

Lucy and L.D. parted when they reached closer to their homes.

Lucy opened the front door and walked straight to the telephone. She was going to tell Clutch about the trip, and ask him if he would drive her to the airport. He would have to cut school as well, but she was positive that he'd do it. She knew that he was hoping that they would start going together. And going to the movies with him had been a lot of fun. Clutch had made her feel grownup and special. It was more than her parents were doing. Actually, if she really thought about it, Clutch was spending more time with her than they were — maybe if he was around more, she'd stop feeling so lonely.

"You're going *where*?" Clutch repeated on the phone.

Lucy told him everything. The silence on the other end told her that she'd really blown his mind.

"You are one *wild* woman," said Clutch.

Lucy giggled.

"What if you get caught?" asked Clutch.

"I won't," said Lucy. She felt ten feet tall.

"Do you want a drive to the airport?" asked Clutch.

"I don't believe it," cried Lucy, "I was just going to ask you that."

"I'll do it, no problem. What are you doing right now?"

"Just hanging around."

"Can I come over?" asked Clutch.

"Sure."

Lucy put the phone down and went upstairs to her room. She wanted to fix herself up. While she was outlining her lips with gloss, she wondered how late her mother would be tonight. The doorbell rang and Lucy raced down.

"Hi," said Clutch, pushing the front door open.

"Boy, you got here so quickly."

"Yeah, the old mobile can burn rubber when it wants to," replied Clutch. He was looking around as he spoke.

"Nobody home but little old me," giggled Lucy.

"Great," said Clutch.

"Follow me," said Lucy, walking towards the den.

"Who's the computer freak?"

Clutch was examining her father's desk, where disks and computer manuals were piled beside his home computer.

"My father."

"Pretty fancy! I guess your folks are loaded."

"Yeah, I guess they do all right. Look, Clutch, I don't really want to talk about them," Lucy said in a grim voice.

"Hey! Don't you get along with them?" Clutch gave Lucy a surprised look.

"No I don't. We all just lead our separate lives. It's no big deal."

"Are you sure?" asked Clutch moving away from the desk and walking up to Lucy.

"Of course, I've been doing it for quite awhile."

Lucy flopped on the sofa and Clutch sat beside her.

"What are they going to say about this trip?"

"Clutch, you didn't come here to talk about my parents." Lucy couldn't keep the annoyance out of her voice.

"No, I came to see you. You got any music in this place?"

"Well, the good stuff is upstairs in my room." Lucy started to rise.

"So let's go to your room," said Clutch, following her.

Walking up to her room with Clutch seemed the most natural thing in the world for Lucy. It was great not to be alone, and her room was the best spot in the entire house. Every inch of wall space was covered with posters. Lucy had hung on to every stuffed toy and doll she had ever got. Part of her room looked like a toy shop. Clutch ignored the stuffed animals and pored through her music, laughing at some of her collection. Then he selected a rock album and jumped on her bed and started dancing. He snatched up Lucy's hairbrush from her dresser, and pretended it was a mike as he sang along with the record. Lucy sat on the floor and laughed.

The music was so loud that neither one of them heard Mrs. Fernandez come home. Clutch was busy doing a complete routine for Lucy, who had her back turned to the doorway.

Suddenly a voice said, "Lucy!"

Clutch froze on the bed, and Lucy swung around.

"Oh, hi! This is Clutch," said Lucy, jumping up.

"Is that your car in the driveway?" asked Mrs. Fernandez.

"Yes, I'm sorry... anyway, I have to go." Clutch scrambled off the bed and almost crashed into Lucy.

He still had Lucy's hairbrush tucked in

the waistband of his jeans. He nodded at Mrs. Fernandez, muttered "see you" to Lucy, and charged out of the room.

"Who is that boy?" said Mrs. Fernandez. She was looking around at Lucy's room.

"He's a friend," said Lucy. She wished she could follow Clutch.

"Do you know he's just walked off with your hairbrush?"

"Yeah, I mean no ... I didn't hear you come in," mumbled Lucy.

"Does he go to Degrassi?" asked her mother.

"Yeah," Lucy lied.

"He looks a little old for junior high."

"What's with all these questions?" said Lucy uncomfortably.

"I don't think your bedroom is a good place to entertain," said Mrs. Fernandez nervously.

"We were just listening to music, Mom."

"Why haven't I seen him before?" persisted her mother.

"Because you aren't here a lot of the time."

Mrs. Fernandez gave a little sigh.

"Lucy, I'm tired, I've had a long day, and coming home to see this friend of yours jumping up and down on your bed doesn't help."

"Okay, so next time we'll stay in the den," offered Lucy.

Mrs. Fernandez walked out of the room.

Lucy looked out of the window. The Clutchmobile had disappeared. Well, at least her mother had met Clutch. One of these days her mother would find out that Clutch was in high school, but for now she seemed to be satisfied. And Lucy had had the small satisfaction of seeing her mother wince at her comment of being away so much.

I've just got be tough, thought Lucy to herself. She flipped on the album she and Clutch were going to play next and decided that she was going to paint her toenails. If you wore a bikini, you had to have painted toenails. They sort of went together. It didn't really matter that her mom had been a little shocked at Clutch. Lucy had her life sorted out for now. Everything was moving along smoothly.

The fuchsia-coloured nail polish sparkled on her toenails. Lucy could almost picture her toes sticking out of the sand in the Bahamas. For a moment she wondered what sort of people she would meet on this vacation. Would there be any kids her age? If she met anyone interesting, she would have to tell them some kind of story — maybe even pretend she wasn't Lucy for awhile.

CHAPTER 8

The next morning, during Mr. Garcia's Math class, Erica leaned over to Lucy. "We have to talk about some things today," she whispered.

"Yes, I know," Lucy whispered back.

"What if your mom calls and wants to speak to you?"

"Quiet, please," said Mr. Garcia, giving both of them a stern look.

Erica drew back, hastily. Mr. Garcia was in a rotten mood already. Nobody had done particularly well on his last Math test. He had asked everyone where they had been all last week — certainly not in his class, paying attention.

Lucy chewed her pen and gave Mr. Garcia what she thought was an attentive look. Inside, Erica's question was tying a knot in her stomach. Would her mom call? She really wasn't the sort to check up; besides, her dad was arriving home on Saturday, and they would be far too busy catching up to worry about her. She couldn't get the thought out of her mind, though. Why had Erica brought it up now?

At lunch period, Lucy finally caught up with the twins and L.D. All three of them were sitting in a huddle, talking.

"Hi," said Lucy. She slid into the chair beside L.D.

"We have some stuff to work out," said L.D. She had a worried look on her face.

"Relax, everything is going to be fine," said Lucy.

"Look, Lucy, you're going to run away. If your mom calls our place looking for you, we could be in *big* trouble." Heather was serious.

"I thought about what you said." Lucy looked at Erica.

"And...?"

"Well, one of you would answer the phone, and the other one would be out... somewhere, with me. That's what you tell her."

"Yeah... I guess that could work," said Erica. She gave Heather a nervous look.

"Okay, " said Heather. She looked at L.D.

"Hey everybody, how about coming over to my place tonight? My mom's going to be out.

And I can model my bikini for all of you," said Lucy. She was dying to show it off.

"Sure," said both the twins.

"I can't make it," said L.D. "I've got some things to do."

"What kind of things?" asked Lucy.

"Cleaning," muttered L.D. She crammed her half-eaten sandwich into her lunch bag.

Lucy watched L.D. pitch her lunch bag into the garbage bin. She hated the fact that part of L.D.'s life was so different from hers. She couldn't help, but she felt bad for L.D. There was nothing she could even say.

When lunch was over and all four of them went for the afternoon classes, Lucy was left feeling uneasy. Something was definitely bothering the twins — Heather in particular. All of a sudden, she was acting like such a wet blanket. Maybe Lucy could find out what was bothering her when they came over. L.D. also had that tight look around her mouth. Wouldn't it be awful if they all backed out of helping her? She had three days left. Nothing was supposed to go wrong now.

Later that evening, when the doorbell rang at Lucy's house, she bounced down to open the door. Lucy had planned a surprise for them. She had put on her bikini, and then covered herself up with her terry bathrobe.

She had also ransacked her mother's jewelry box and found a silver chain which she had draped around her midriff. It looped around her waist twice and dangled over her navel. She had also found four thin, silver bracelets which she had pushed all the way up her arms. The finishing touch was a silver headband which pushed her hair back so it tumbled over one shoulder.

Lucy opened the door. The twins walked in. Lucy shut the door after them and led them into the living room. Leaning against the door frame, she opened her bathrobe, said "Ta daaa," and shrugged off the robe. The robe slid down to the floor, and two pairs of eyes goggled at her.

"Oh boy, Lucy, you look sensational," breathed Erica.

"That's a fabulous bikini," said Heather.

"I can just see you, you're never going to come back." Erica shook her head in amazement.

"Does this mean you approve?" said Lucy mischievously.

"Turn around," ordered Heather.

Lucy swiveled around on her heels. The twins just stared at her. Lucy looked like an absolute fashion plate — something out of a slick magazine advertisement. Also, the amazing thing was that she didn't look fifteen. She looked much older. I'll never ever look like that, thought Heather enviously. I'm going to go on a diet right now for summer, Erica thought to herself. It may kill me, but I want to look just like that.

"It looks all right, doesn't it?" asked Lucy anxiously. They were so quiet.

"Lucy, somebody is going to flip for you on that island," announced Erica.

"Great," said Lucy, twirling around like a ballerina, "I'm ready for an adventure."

"I wonder what it's going to look like when it gets wet?" mused Heather.

"Wet!" shouted Lucy. All three of them burst out laughing.

"I want to see everything that you're taking," said Erica.

They walked up to her bedroom. Lucy pulled her duffle bag from under her bed.

"Are you taking that disgusting old thing?" asked Erica.

"I couldn't find a smaller suitcase," explained Lucy.

"We've got some bags at home," offered Heather.

Lucy stood there for a moment with the duffle bag in her hands. Despite what she had felt earlier on, she wanted to take it with her. In three days' time she was going to be doing things she had never done before —

flying away to a brand new place. The old duffle bag had something reassuring about it. It was familiar, and it was hers. She didn't want the others to know, but she needed a little security.

"This bag," said Lucy, flinging it on the bed, "is going to take a vacation. It's going to the Bahamas."

"Well, I hope you don't wind up looking like a runaway kid," muttered Heather.

"No chance of that." Lucy whipped out a pair of sunglasses and a low-brimmed hat from the top of the bag. She put on the sunglasses and tilted the hat over one eye. She pulled on a long, knit skirt and a loose, floppy top.

Suddenly the doorbell rang.

"Oh God, I hope it isn't my mother," cried Lucy. She peeked out the bedroom window.

The twins crowded behind her. Lucy couldn't see her mother's car.

"Want me to check?" asked Erica.

"Yeah, I need to get out of this stuff," said Lucy, jerking off the hat and sunglasses.

Erica pounded down the stairs. Lucy ripped off the skirt and pulled on her jeans. Heather quickly pushed the duffle bag under Lucy's bed. Then they heard Erica laughing hysterically. Another voice asked what was so funny.

"It's only L.D.," cried Lucy.

"L.D.," yelled Heather.

"I'm going to kill you, L.D." Lucy collapsed on her bed.

"What's going on?" L.D. walked into Lucy's room with Erica.

"I thought you couldn't make it."

"Well, I just zipped through everything. I guess I really wanted to see the bikini."

"You almost gave me a heart attack!" exclaimed Lucy. She jumped up from her bed.

"Where'd you get the skirt?" asked L.D. It didn't look one bit like Lucy.

"What do you mean?"

"I just.... " L.D.'s voice trailed off defensively.

"I know what you mean," bristled Lucy. "I'm sick and tired of your policeman look. First you arrive and scare me to death and then I have to put up with all these questions."

"Oh, don't be such a pain, I didn't mean anything," L.D. snapped back.

"Don't fight, guys... you're best friends," wailed Erica.

"Nobody's fighting," murmured L.D.

"Well, just for your information, L.D., it's one of my mom's summer skirts, and she's not going to miss it," announced Lucy smugly.

"Okay, okay. Now where's the great

bikini?" said L.D. She flashed her sunniest smile at Lucy.

When Lucy pulled off her jeans and top, she still wore the bikini underneath.

"You look sensational," whispered L.D.

"You really think so?" asked Lucy. She realized how much she wanted L.D.'s support, and how glad she was that L.D. had decided to come after all.

"Lucy, what are you going to do all by yourself, for three days and three nights?" asked Erica.

"I'm going to be on the beach all day and I'm going to go dancing at night." Lucy wiggled her shoulders.

"Yeah, but how is it going to feel, to do it alone?" persisted Erica.

"She's going to meet all sorts of people," suggested L.D.

"With that bikini, you're going to be swarmed the first day," Heather smiled.

Lucy flashed Heather a smile right back. It seemed that whatever was worrying Heather had worked itself out. Lucy felt terrific. Maybe one of these days, all four of them could go on a trip and lie on the sand somewhere, wearing bikinis and driving the guys wild.

The telephone rang. It was Lucy's mom. What was Lucy up to? Were there any messages for her? Lucy chatted glibly for a few minutes and hung up the phone. The twins were ready to leave, but L.D. hung around. Lucy shut the door behind the twins, and turned around. She said to L.D.

"I'm glad Heather is over her snit, or whatever."

"She got cold feet."

"What do you mean?"

"Well, she thought that... maybe you were doing something wrong... and we were helping you."

"What do you think?"

"I couldn't do it... it would just kill my dad. I guess it takes a lot of nerve." L.D looked uncomfortable.

Lucy kept quiet. How could she tell L.D. that she didn't think her parents cared about her? As for nerve, well she was proving it to herself that she had plenty of that.

"I'm doing it, L.D.," said Lucy. She looked L.D. squarely in the face. "And if anyone wants to back out, I can do it — all on my own."

"Nobody's backing out," said L.D. fiercely, "I'm just worried. Clutch is driving you. Anything could happen."

"Come on L.D., you're just saying that because you don't really like him," accused Lucy.

"You don't understand, Lucy. All right, *let* Clutch drive."

Lucy turned away from L.D. feeling miserable all of a sudden. Why was L.D. being such a pain about Clutch? The twins were fine with her. Nobody gave her the impression that what she was doing was wrong. They had all been excited, admiring her clothes and even envying her.

"Lucy," said L.D. putting on her jacket and getting ready to leave, "my dad keeps lecturing me about stuff like honesty and values. It gets a bit confusing but I just don't believe in letting a friend down."

"Thanks L.D.," whispered Lucy, "you're a real pal."

CHAPTER 9

The next day, when Lucy walked home after school, she found her mom's car in the driveway. What was her mom doing home at 3:30 in the afternoon? Lucy quickened her steps. For one panic-stricken moment she thought that maybe she had forgotten to push the duffle bag under her bed. What if her mom had walked into her room and found it?

Lucy opened the front door quietly and slipped inside. There was no sign of her mother downstairs. Lucy threw her jacket and school bag on the kitchen table and headed up the stairs.

"Lucy, is that you?" called her mother.

"Hi," said Lucy, walking towards her mom's room — that's where the voice had come from.

"I took some time off," said her mom. "I've asked them to forward my calls here."

Lucy looked at her mom, stretched out on the bed. She had kicked off her shoes, but she was still all dressed up. Her briefcase was lying beside her, open. Lucy could see that there was some mail lying next to the case.

"Lucy, do you still have my Visa card?" asked her mom.

Lucy gave her mother a blank stare. Inside a voice said, this is it, she knows, it's all over.

"Lucy, where is my card?" repeated her mother.

"Oh — that!... I got the ballet tickets on it, remember? I guess it's here somewhere," stammered Lucy.

"Well, find it please, and bring it to me."

Lucy went to her bedroom. The card was lying in the top drawer of her dresser. Her mother just wanted it back, that was all. She found the card and headed back. She had to be very cool about this.

"Here it is," said Lucy.

"Thank you," said her mom, reaching for her handbag.

Lucy watched her mother replace the card in her wallet. There were many other cards inside the billfold — a small row of them.

Boy, thought Lucy to herself, adults really have it made. They walk around with all these credit cards and can do anything they want. Kids, on the other hand, have to do what their parents say, just because they don't have money. It made her feel resentful.

"Come and sit with me for awhile, and tell me what's happening at school," said her mom, patting the bed and giving Lucy a warm smile.

"Sure."

Lucy peeled off her shoes and socks and flopped on the edge of the bed.

"That's a set of colourful toes," said her mom, looking at Lucy's feet.

Lucy curled her toes involuntarily. The bright, fuchsia-coloured nail polish was like a neon sign. She'd never painted her toes like this, and her mom was bound to make something of it.

"Getting rid of the February blahs?" asked her mom, giving Lucy a girlish, conspiratorial smile.

Lucy grinned at her mom in reply, and dangled her feet over the edge of the bed, where they couldn't be seen.

"So tell me, what's happening this weekend?"

"I'm going to be with the twins, and there's a birthday party, and we have lots of running around to do for it." Lucy could hear her voice rising with nervousness.

"Well, you certainly sound very excited." Her mom gave her a penetrating look.

"It's going to be like a three-day holiday. You know — a break from school."

"How did that Math test go last week?"

"Lousy."

"Do you think you need a tutor, Lucy?" asked her mom.

"No, I just need to do some catching up — that's all." Lucy tried to shrug it off.

"Well, if you have Monday off, you could do some studying."

The telephone rang. Her mom reached across to her bedside table and picked it up. Lucy watched her mother switch to a real estate agent instantly. She sat up, pulled her briefcase closer to her, and pulled out some papers. Lucy felt as though the rug had been pulled out from under her. She flashed a murderous look at her mother's briefcase. The fleeting moment of flopping on the bed with her mother felt good. Why couldn't it have lasted just a little longer? Why couldn't her mother have said, I'll call back, I'm with my daughter right now.

Lucy felt herself curling up on the bed, her body folded into a tight, lonely huddle. Eventually she slid off the edge of the bed and walked out of the room. Her mother didn't even look up.

Lucy walked down to the kitchen to fix herself a snack. Apparently her mother had every intention of playing mom today. She had even come home with Lucy's favourite dessert. A Dufflet's carrot cake sat on the top shelf of the refrigerator. Lucy cut a huge slice of cake and poured herself a glass of milk. This was her favourite combination, even her dad loved it.

Lucy thought of her father. He was such a blur at times. She remembered how hurt and quiet he had been during that whole shoplifting episode. It had been such a rotten time for all of them. And after, when her parents had made an effort to spend some time with her, Lucy couldn't be sure of their motives. Did they really care about her, or was she just being supervised? Then, before anything was worked out, her parents got involved in their jobs all over again. All the plans to do things together just kept getting postponed. Lucy knew they were in a rut again.

As she munched her carrot cake, Lucy knew that she wasn't feeling as excited as she ought to be about her trip — that old, dark shadow was beginning to creep up. Her mother had been so wonderfully innocent about everything. That should have made her feel confident, but even something as simple as eating the carrot cake was painful. Instead of delicious bites of carrot cake sliding down her throat, sticky bits of guilt were getting in the way.

L.D. telephoned a few minutes later. Lucy was grateful to be rescued from her troubling thoughts.

"How's it going?"

"Everything's fine," replied Lucy, pushing the plate of half-eaten carrot cake away.

"You know there's an airport bus that leaves from the Royal York Hotel."

"L.D., Clutch won't let me down," came Lucy's irate response.

"It's good to have a back-up plan."

"Nothing is going to go wrong!" screamed Lucy into the telephone.

"What's the matter, Lucy?" asked a voice behind her.

Lucy jumped. Her mother was standing there with her shoes on, holding her briefcase in one hand and the car keys in the other.

"Honey... "

"It's okay, L.D. and I just have a problem." Lucy eyed her mother nervously, and seeing the car keys in her mother's hand, she sighed. "Yeah, I know Mom, you have to go."

"I think Daddy is going to call from San

Francisco tonight," said her mother.

"Just a minute, L.D." Lucy held the phone to her chest.

"Have a nice long chat with him. You can have that microwave lasagna for dinner."

"Sure."

"I don't think I'll be late."

"Okay." Lucy waggled her fingers at her mother and lifted the phone back up to her ear.

"And Lucy..."

"What?"

"Do some Math. It won't kill you," suggested her mother.

Lucy nodded vaguely and waved again as her mother went out the front door.

"Are you still there?" asked L.D.

"Wanna go out?" said Lucy. There was no way she wanted to sit at home eating microwave lasagna and doing Math.

"I think my dad's going to give me the 'school nights' lecture if I ask him."

L.D. didn't sound too hopeful. They talked for a few minutes about the trip, and when Lucy hung up, she knew exactly who would rescue her. She called Clutch. Twenty minutes later he arrived. Lucy locked the front door and looked down the street nervously. As usual there was music blaring out of the Clutchmobile. Clutch was looking quite spiffy. He was wearing a leather jacket with all sorts of pins on it.

"Let's go, babe," said Clutch, leaning over and shutting Lucy's door.

"Where are we going?" asked Lucy. She was beginning to feel a lot better.

"There's this new club on Sherbourne," said Clutch, giving Lucy a quick once-over.

"I won't be able to get in."

"Sure you will. I've got some fake I.D.," Clutch said, smiling. "Just put on some... lipstick."

Lucy rummaged in her purse and dug out a lipstick. Well, maybe this was a good time to test how old she could look. The twins and L.D. had assured her that she could get away with a lot. It's time to find out, thought Lucy, outlining her lips in bright red.

Clutch pulled into an alley and parked the car. He reached into his pocket and produced a little wad of fake I.Ds. They had all sorts of names on them. Kids would lose them, or just sell them.

It was a wild place all right. The walls were painted black with some far-out graphics in red and purple splashed all over them. And the people going in were definitely older kids. Clutch walked through the front door holding Lucy's hand. Nobody said a word, and they found a little table.

"Clutch," whispered Lucy, "I really don't want to get into any drinking."

"One beer... that's all."

"What'll it be?" A waitress had materialized at Lucy's elbow.

"Er... I'll have—"

"Got any I.D.?" The waitress's smile was a mile wide.

"Two Cokes," blurted Clutch.

The waitress raised one eyebrow sardonically and sauntered off. Lucy stared at Clutch. He crinkled up his eyes and smiled at her.

"You lost your nerve, Lucy Fernandez."

"I did not."

"You hesitated, and she knew," replied Clutch.

"So why did you chicken out?" Lucy was annoyed by the superior expression on Clutch's face.

"Oh, I thought I'd keep you company, you know, do whatever pleases you."

"Thanks," said Lucy softly, wanting so much to believe him.

"You know what they drink on those islands, don't you?"

"What?"

"*Is-a-land* rum," sang Clutch, putting on a West Indian accent.

"So I'll drink it there," giggled Lucy.

89

"I'd like to see that," replied Clutch, leaning closer to Lucy.

"But you won't. I'll be gone. And you'll be right here," said Lucy flicking her fingertips under his nose.

"Oh yeah, but I have ways of catching up," said Clutch.

"Do you have any brothers and sisters, Clutch?"

"Yup, I have two older brothers. What about you?"

"I'm an only child," said Lucy, softly.

"Ever get lonesome?" asked Clutch.

"Sort of..." Lucy looked away.

"Not anymore, I'm going to be your shadow."

"Okay," laughed Lucy, "that's great."

"So what did your mom say about me?"

"She wasn't crazy about you dancing on my bed."

"What else?"

"Nothing else... I don't think she cares about who I see — after all I'm going to be sixteen," replied Lucy.

"Hey, do you want a driving lesson in the old Dominion Store parking lot?"

"Clutch," squealed Lucy, "would you really?"

"Follow me," said Clutch pushing back his chair and holding out his hand for Lucy.

The driving lesson lasted about thirty seconds. Lucy was terrified. She had said yes because it seemed to be a very grown-up thing to do. But all of a sudden the car rolled forward and she didn't know what to do next. When she remembered, she hit the brake so hard that Clutch banged his head. Lucy told Clutch to drive again, but he wasn't ready to go home.

"Let's go to Lick's." Clutch slid behind the wheel and started the car.

"That's all the way to the Beaches. Clutch, I want to go home."

"Aw, come on, Lucy. You told me your mom was pretty cool."

"I want to go home, Clutch," Lucy repeated.

"Hey, we haven't had any fun yet," protested Clutch.

"I've had plenty. Besides, I've got some Math homework."

"I can get us there and back in a flash." Clutch stepped on the accelerator.

"Stop it, Clutch! Take me home!" Lucy screamed.

Clutch slammed on the brakes and the Clutchmobile squealed to a halt. Then without a word, he drove Lucy home.

CHAPTER 10

Lucy let herself into the dark house. She could hear Clutch pulling away from the driveway, and for a moment she huddled against the door. It was almost nine o'clock. She had got home before her mother, but she was a bundle of nerves. Driving lessons would have to wait for awhile. She was still quivering with the aftershock.

Lucy walked through the house turning all the lights on. She wondered what Clutch would think of her. Would he speak to her again? But it wasn't all her fault. Clutch had a way of pulling surprises. She didn't want to tell him that she just didn't want any trouble two days before her trip. Clutch, thought Lucy, I love your crazy, daring side, but sometimes you go too far and you scare me.

All of a sudden she realized she was hungry and remembered what her mother had said about dinner. Lucy opened the freezer and took out the lasagna, and put the frozen block into the microwave oven and punched out the time. She stared at the lasagna twirling around behind the small glass pane. The rotating casserole dish made Lucy see herself spinning around on a golden beach. The beach was in the Bahamas. She was two days away from her fantasy getaway where the most wonderful things were going to happen. The best part was that all the messy parts of her life would be left behind. No more looking at glossy magazines and imagining that glamourous things only happened to other people.

The telephone rang in shrill, harsh tones. Lucy resented the intrusion on her fantasy. She picked up the receiver reluctantly.

"Hi... Lucy?" It was her father.

"Daddy!" said Lucy.

"Where is everyone? I've been calling all evening." Her father sounded annoyed.

"Oh, Mom's at work, and I was... up in my room with the radio on."

"But I've called at least five times! Is everything all right?" There was an unmistakable note of concern in his voice.

"Just great," said Lucy quickly.

"What do you want from San Francisco?"

"Oh, anything."

"Is everything all right?" asked her father again.

"Yes."

"When I get back, we'll go out for a super-special dinner somewhere."

"Okay."

"Tell Mom. Well... I'll be home on Saturday."

"Okay."

"Well, I have some people waiting here, I'm late already. Bye honey."

"Daddy... " started Lucy, but he had already hung up.

Lucy stared at the telephone receiver in her hand. She wanted to smash it at something, but she made herself replace it, quietly. She didn't even know what she wanted to say to her father, but he had made sure she didn't get to say it anyway. She was angry with herself. When her father mentioned going out for a fancy dinner she had felt like bursting into tears. She couldn't understand why. Even when he had asked if everything was all right, she'd had that same feeling. Miles away, in San Francisco, her father was trying to play Dad, but it hadn't worked. What would have happened if she had answered, no, nothing is all right? Would he have taken the first plane home? Why were tears rolling down her face?

Stop it, Lucy Fernandez, said the other Lucy — the tough, cool Lucy. You're not going to fall apart now. All you're doing is bailing out, taking a hike from parents who are never around, and the boring scene at Degrassi. Well, she hated boring old routines and not having some kind of excitement. Now that she had reached out all by herself and found an adventure she could not get teary-eyed. It just wouldn't do.

Lucy cut herself a piece of lasagna and walked into the family room. She switched on the television and sat down to eat her dinner. *Dallas* was on, and it was good enough company for her. What was even better was the commercial that popped up halfway through. A beautiful couple was in the middle of a romantic holiday in some place called Tobago. It looked just like the pictures of the Bahamas. Lucy's toes curled with excitement. "That's going to be me," she said loudly in the empty house.

After *Dallas* was over, Lucy flicked around for something interesting to watch, but there was nothing on. A few minutes later she heard the front door opening and her mother walked in. Lucy switched the T.V. off. She knew that her school bag was lying unopened in the kitchen. There was no sign of any homework being done anywhere.

"Hi Lucy. How was the lasagna?" called her mom.

Lucy went into the kitchen. Her mother was cutting a grapefruit in half.

"Are you still on that diet?" asked Lucy. She moved casually to block her mother's view of the chair on which her unopened school bag lay.

Her mother smiled at her and nodded.

"Oh, Daddy called."

"What did he say?"

"He's going to be home on the weekend — Saturday."

Her mother dug a spoon into the grapefruit. "And you're going to be away. You know, honey, maybe you should be home on Sunday."

Lucy looked at her mother with a horrified expression on her face. Was this some kind of monstrous joke?

"Well, have I said something so terrible?" exclaimed her mother.

"No," blurted Lucy. "Mom, we've made this plan weeks ago. I can't let everyone down."

"All right. All right." Her mother put up her hands in surrender.

"I'm going to see Dad on Monday, and you guys will get a chance to be by yourselves."

"Lucy," said her mother with an amused smile on her face, "thank you."

Lucy could barely control her sigh of relief. She studied her mother apprehensively. Was she going to come up with another disastrous idea? But her mother seemed to be concentrating on removing neat little sections of grapefruit. The telephone rang, and Lucy moved with the distraction immediately. She turned around, grabbed the school bag and dashed out of the kitchen. As she was flying up the stairs, she heard her mother shout, "It's for you, Lucy."

Lucy reached her room and flung down her school bag. She picked up the phone, and when she heard her mother hang up, she flopped on her bed.

"Hi, are you all ready?"

It was Erica. Lucy was glad that somebody had called.

"Yeah, but you won't believe what just happened," said Lucy. "My mom thought I should come home on Sunday."

"You're kidding!"

"I just managed to scrape out of that one," replied Lucy.

"Boy, you must have nerves of steel or something."

"I just have to play it cool."

"Well, if anyone is cool, it's you Lucy,"

Erica giggled.

"I just want you and Heather to be cool about the whole thing too." Lucy spoke hesitantly.

"Don't worry," reassured Erica, "I think we've worked everything out."

"And if things get too hot, you can just say you don't know where I am."

"I don't know if Heather would go for that, but I'll convince her," promised Erica.

Lucy sighed. So there was still trouble with Heather. In front of Lucy she said one thing, but in front of her twin she said something else. Why was she being so difficult? Lucy's mom would never check up, and if she did call, the solution was simple.

"Lucy, are you there?" Erica sounded concerned.

"I'm here."

"Don't worry. It's scary as hell, but just think the day after tomorrow you're going to be *away*!"

"Do you want to come to the airport?" asked Lucy. Erica was such a cheerful person, she thought — just the sort of person to have along on the ride.

"With Clutch?" Erica was teasing her.

"Yes, with Clutch." Lucy felt herself tensing up.

"Are you sure I wouldn't be interrupting?"

"Don't be a pain, Erica. I get that from L.D. all the time."

"How are we going to work it out?"

Lucy told her. Clutch would meet them outside the school at two. It would mean cutting last period, but Clutch could probably have them back by four. Once Lucy checked in at the airport, they couldn't stay anyway. She didn't tell Erica that she didn't know if Clutch would even call her again.

"I'll speak to Heather," promised Erica.

Lucy knew Erica had a way of convincing Heather. It was all tied up with being a twin. Lucy had always envied the twins. They were a pair, even when they did different things. It must be so wonderful to have a sister — a sort of ready-made friend who was always there for you. The best part was that you were never alone.

Suddenly Lucy realized that her mother was standing in her doorway.

"Are you still on the phone?" said her mother. "It's almost 10:30."

Lucy whispered, "Bye," and hung up.

"No, I'm off," she said hurriedly.

"You have all the time on the weekend for gossip."

"I'm going to bed."

"Do I have to drop you off at the twins on Friday evening?" asked her mother.

"No, no... I'm going back with them after school."

"What about your things, your clothes and... toothbrush?" her mother had a puzzled look on her face.

"Oh, I'll put everything in my old camp duffle and take it to school."

"Do you need anything else?"

This is the time, Lucy said to herself. I've got to ask her for some money. Tomorrow will be too late.

"Mom, do you think I could borrow some money?" asked Lucy. She could feel her entire face heat up.

"How much?"

"Fifty dollars," said Lucy.

"What for?" exclaimed her mother.

Lucy had rehearsed the story in her mind. Just let her believe it, she prayed.

"The twins' grandmother said she'd make us dresses for graduation. She's coming to their place this weekend to measure us and stuff," said Lucy.

"So is this money for sewing or for the fabric?" asked her mother.

"Both," said Lucy promptly.

"That's a wonderful deal," replied her mom.

"She's making some wild outfits for us," smiled Lucy.

She knew the battle had been won.

CHAPTER 11

Lucy squeezed some shampoo into the palm of her hand and rubbed it in her hair. It was Wednesday morning and she had woken up early, so she decided to wash her hair. She knew that the next time she would do this it certainly wouldn't be in her own bathroom. "One more day," she sang to herself under the shower. Tomorrow is Thursday, and Friday — I'm off.

She could hardly wait to get to school and tell L.D. that even the money problem had been solved. She wasn't going to tell anyone what she had told her mother — that was her business, but she had worked out everything — that was what counted. The most important thing that remained was to find out if she could still rely on Clutch. Last night hadn't ended so well. Would he still be annoyed with her?

When Lucy got to school, she found a buzz of conversation going on at the lockers. Some of the kids were talking about graduation in June. Everybody wanted to be on the graduation committee. Lucy couldn't understand how anyone could get excited about June. It was so far away. She moved away from the little huddle of people feeling curiously detached, and quite superior.

"You know," said L.D. catching up with Lucy in first period, "I woke up this morning and realized there's one more day left."

"I know, I can hardly wait," replied Lucy.

"I just hope everything is going to work out," said L.D.

Lucy flashed L.D. an indulgent smile. L.D. was such a worry wart, but that was all right because it was L.D.'s way of showing that she cared. At least she was honest about her feelings. For one crazy moment Lucy felt like standing up in class and telling everyone — look at me, I'm going to do something truly fantastic. Everyone would drool with envy. It would be a great feeling, and it would make that dark shadow disappear permanently. Good feelings had a way of chasing away problems.

The rest of the day whizzed by in a blur. Lucy found herself drifting in and out of clas-

ses, locked in her own private world. She
didn't even bother writing down homework
assignments. All that would just have to
wait. Maybe, I'll never come back, thought
Lucy to herself — just become a beach bum
— maybe find a job. She had heard about
kids doing that. All sorts of things were possible.

After school, Lucy walked outside with
L.D. A big surprise was waiting for her.
Clutch was sitting in his car across the
street. It's all right, Lucy thought to herself.
If he was angry he wouldn't show up. There
were a few kids around his car. The
Clutchmobile drew lots of attention. Turning
sixteen and learning how to drive was a top
priority for everyone, even though most of
them wouldn't be able to get their hands on
a car until they were older.

"Is he waiting for you?" L.D. nudged Lucy.

"I don't know." Lucy gave a nervous grin
and fluffed her hair with her fingers.

"Well, I guess I'd better get lost," sighed
L.D.

"Do you mind?" asked Lucy.

"Why should I care? He's your friend."

"L.D., he really is a pretty neat person. I'm
just getting to know him." Lucy tried to
defend Clutch.

"Just make sure he's here early on

103

Friday."

Lucy watched L.D. walk away. L.D. wasn't prepared to change her opinion about Clutch, and that was that. Oh well, maybe that's the way it was meant to be, thought Lucy to herself as she walked towards the Clutchmobile. Two girls who she didn't know were leaning on the car talking to Clutch. Clutch was throwing back his head and laughing, and she knew could tell that the girls thought he was pretty cute. They had silly, flirty looks on their faces. They kept glancing at her as she came closer.

"Am I interrupting something?" asked Lucy.

"No, I've been waiting for you," replied Clutch promptly.

"Excuse me," said Lucy, brushing past the blonde girl who had draped herself over the passenger door.

The girl moved back from the door slowly. She gave Lucy a silly grin and stood there watching her get into the car. Clutch started the car. The girl looked at Clutch and said, "Great talking to you. See you again, okay?"

Clutch flashed a smile at her and reversed the car. Lucy could feel a prickle of irritation all over.

"Hi," said Clutch, looking at her out of the corner of his eye.

"Who was that?" asked Lucy.

"I don't know," shrugged Clutch.

"Oh, really...." Lucy's voice dripped with sarcasm.

"Honest," replied Clutch with a straight face, and then he started laughing.

Lucy started giggling as well. The blonde girl was so obvious about her interest in Clutch, and she was really mad at Lucy. Clutch seemed to think it was pretty funny. Actually it was, but only because she knew that Clutch had come for her.

"Clutch, I'm sorry about last night...."

"It's okay. I thought maybe your mother isn't as cool as you make her out to be."

"Something like that..." mumbled Lucy.

"Don't sweat it, Lucy." Clutch flashed a warm smile at her.

Lucy smiled right back at Clutch. Everything is going to work out, sang a little voice inside her head.

"You know, I've been thinking about your er... getaway," Clutch said very slowly.

"What about it?"

"Do you want some company?"

"What do you mean?"

"Well," said Clutch, "I wouldn't mind going with you."

Lucy gave Clutch a startled look. She didn't know what to say. How could Clutch come with her? They weren't going to a rock concert. She was going on a vacation package that had been booked and paid for. No one had said anything about Clutch coming on the trip.

"I have this savings account for my university, and I could draw some money out of it," added Clutch.

Lucy felt a sense of panic. She swallowed hard. Clutch was waiting for her to say something, and she was sitting here like a dummy. It was beginning to sound just like last night.

"So what do you say?" asked Clutch, pulling up neatly into her driveway.

"Clutch, I don't know... this is my trip... I mean... I really want to do this by myself."

"Yeah, but think what a great time we'd have together," Clutch flashed her a sexy look.

Oh no, thought Lucy to herself. This is going to be like last night all over again. Clutch was ready to latch on to her adventure, and she didn't want that. How was she going to tell him without hurting his feelings? He was looking at her with an expectant smile. Lucy took a deep breath, and turned to him.

"Clutch, I don't know how to say this, but I'm doing this alone."

Clutch didn't say anything, and the silence in the car was deafening. Lucy looked ahead miserably. Clutch was miffed, she could tell. Now he was thinking of some way to get out of it.

"I like you very much," Lucy said in a soft voice.

Clutch looked out of the window with a moody expression on his face.

"It's just that I hadn't planned on going with anyone," continued Lucy.

"Sure." Clutch turned and looked at her. "Okay, I get the message."

"Do you want to come in for awhile?" asked Lucy. She wanted to make up for the awkward moment.

"Nah... I don't think so...."

"Oh Clutch," said Lucy, "I'm sorry...."

She got out of the car, and shut the door. She looked at Clutch, feeling embarrassed. Clutch looked fidgety, as though he wanted to be anywhere but here. He gave her a wobbly smile and backed the car down the driveway. Lucy waved to him, and stood for a minute watching the Clutchmobile roar down the street and disappear at the corner. Nothing had been said about the drive to the airport. Lucy didn't know what to think. How was she going to ask Clutch about it again? Somehow she had to do it, and very soon.

Lucy walked up the front steps of her house. She was glad to be home and by herself. What on earth had made Clutch come up with his last minute scheme? She started to feel guilty. Then she pushed the feeling away. What was Clutch thinking anyway? Was he always going to be like this — pushing her to do things she didn't want to do? If she hadn't told him about the trip, then this awkward situation wouldn't have arisen. She was probably giving Clutch the wrong impression. Maybe L.D. was right about Clutch.

Lucy opened the fridge and picked at the carrot cake sitting on the top shelf. She pulled out a Coke and walked upstairs to her bedroom. This was the time to do a last minute check on her luggage. Erica had told her that she better take some sun block with her. Even though Lucy was a shade darker than the twins, she did burn in the sun. Erica had also suggested that she should find a pair of sunglasses. "Great disguise" was what Erica had said, and Lucy had agreed with her. There were little odds and ends that had to be added to the duffle bag, and she wanted to do it before her mom came home from work.

Pulling out the bag from under her bed, Lucy emptied all the contents on her bed.

Then she started to neatly fold everything —
three pairs of shorts with tank tops, one
bikini, two skirts and a wraparound jersey
dress. Lucy realized that she had forgotten
underwear, so she went to her dresser to get
some — that's when she thought of sandals.
She didn't have any. Her last pair of summer
sandals had worn out, and she had thrown
them away. There was no time to get anything else, so she slipped in her pink Keds.
They would have to do. Besides, everyone
probably went barefoot on the island.

She also found her sunglasses. They
weren't the really big, mysterious kind, but
the kinky Queen Street ones with red plastic
rims. Lucy put them on and looked at herself
in the mirror. They would look ghastly with
her bikini. She would take them along, just
in case, but she was positive she wouldn't
wear them.

Twenty minutes later the bag was packed
for the last time, and Lucy decided to call
L.D. and tell her that she was absolutely
ready. She wasn't prepared for L.D.'s question.

"I've been thinking about this trip," said
L.D. "Listen have you got a passport or some
kind of identification?"

Lucy jerked the phone away from her ear
in terror. She didn't know whether she even

had a passport!

"Well, do you?" L.D.'s voice boomed out.

"I don't know... Oh L.D., *everything* is going wrong — first Clutch and now this." Lucy's voice rose hysterically.

"Well you'd better call that travel agent and find out — and what did that creep do?"

Lucy couldn't reply. This wasn't the time for explanations, and she couldn't bear L.D. saying I told you so to her.

"Well, are you going to tell me?" demanded L.D.

"Look, I've got to get off the phone and call the travel agency," blurted Lucy.

"Lucy," yelled L.D., "don't you dare hang up... what has Clutch done?"

"L.D. I can't talk just now," replied Lucy, slamming the phone down.

CHAPTER 12

Lucy rummaged through her father's desk drawer, carefully examining everything. This was where her parents kept important papers. There was no sign of any passports. She had telephoned the agency, but it was closed, so she had charged down to the den. The large desk, with all its drawers, had to contain something. All she found were bills and stubs of cheque books and papers about the house. There was one white envelope with "Lucy" scrawled on it. She opened it quickly. The folded square of paper turned out to be her birth certificate. Lucy slipped it back in the envelope. Then she walked back up to her room with the envelope, and tucked it into her bag.

She dialed L.D.'s number with shaky fingers.

"I've got a copy of my birth certificate."

"Lucy, I think you better call the travel agency and check," said L.D.

"They're closed."

"Oh boy!"

"I'll do it first thing tomorrow," said Lucy.

"Ready to tell me about Clutch?" prompted L.D.

"It's nothing."

"Lucy, are you getting serious about him?"

"Yes and no," said Lucy. She might as well be honest.

"What's that supposed to mean?" L.D. sounded indignant.

"Just cool it, L.D. It's nothing I can't handle."

"You know he's crazy."

"Yeah," said Lucy. "That's why I like him." She realized it was true, even though his craziness sometimes frightened her.

"Oh, Lucy." L.D. sounded serious. "Why do you think he's called Mr. Action?"

"Because he's so exciting, and everyone's jealous," cut in Lucy.

L.D. was silent for a moment. "Okay Lucy, I'm just warning you," she said.

"L.D., I don't want to hear anything about Clutch right now, okay?" pleaded Lucy.

"Okay... I get the message... I'll see you tomorrow." L.D. hung up.

That was the second time today someone

had said "I get the message", thought Lucy, but they hadn't, really. She looked at the birth certificate in her hand. It said that she was born in New York, but since then her parents had moved to Canada. Lucy remembered her father telling her that she was a Canadian citizen. Did this mean that she had a passport somewhere? She would have to ask her mother, and do it without arousing any suspicion.

Lucy paced around the house, chewing her fingernails. It was a horrible feeling to have an unexpected hitch at the last moment. Why hadn't anyone thought of this before?

When her mother arrived home, Lucy had to restrain herself from jumping up and asking her. She knew she had to play it very cool.

"Hello, darling. It's been a long day... I'm quite ready for the weekend," said her mother.

"Hi, Mom," said Lucy.

"Just give me a minute to change, and then I'll get dinner going."

Lucy trailed behind her mother, following her up the stairs. Her mom slipped off her shoes, and hung up her suit jacket.

"Mom, do we have passports?" blurted Lucy. She couldn't wait any longer.

Her mother looked startled by the question. "Well, Daddy and I do, but we haven't actually got around to getting you one. Why do you ask?"

Lucy stared at her mother. A million thoughts were racing through her, each one worse than the last.

"Are you planning a trip?" Her mom had a wry smile on her face.

Lucy jumped, as though she had received an electric shock. "What's the matter, Lucy?"

Be cool, thought Lucy. "Oh nothing," she said. "It's just that somebody at school was talking about it, and I wondered... whether I had one." She tried to sound as nonchalant as possible.

"Is one of your friends going on a trip?"

"Yeah, I think somewhere in the Caribbean. You know, one of those islands."

"Lucky girl. I wouldn't mind running off to a sun spot right now," said her mother.

Lucy looked at her mother. Did she suspect anything? But her mom was busy pulling on a velour track suit, and seemed to have dismissed the conversation.

"Can you travel without a passport?" asked Lucy.

"Sometimes. What do you want for dinner, Lucy?"

"How about one of your salads?" suggested

114

Lucy automatically. Food was the last thing on her mind.

"All right, let's go down and see what we can find." Her mom moved towards the door.

Lucy, stayed in her mom's room for awhile. She couldn't ask anything else. That would definitely get her mother thinking. She had come so close to the truth already. This was getting pretty dangerous. Her stomach was in knots and she felt her throat getting dry. She was no closer to knowing whether she needed a passport or not. Lucy called L.D. on her mother's phone.

"L.D.," whispered Lucy, "I'm going crazy, I don't know what to do."

"Is your mom there?"

"Yeah, I mean no, I mean she's downstairs."

"Well, what did she say?" asked L.D. impatiently.

"I don't have a passport, but you don't need it all the time."

"Oh *boy*. Lucy, you'd better make sure."

"How?" Lucy whispered fiercely.

"Lucy." Her mother's voice floated up the stairs.

"I've got to go, L.D.," said Lucy hurriedly.

"But what are you going to do?"

"I don't know," moaned Lucy into the phone, "I just don't know."

Lucy walked downstairs slowly. Maybe the twins or even Clutch knew a way of finding out tonight what she needed to know. She certainly wasn't ready for a chatty little dinner with her mom. In the kitchen her mom was frying omelettes in a pan. A large bowl of salad was resting on the table.

"I'm making us cheese omelettes to go with the salad," smiled her mom.

Lucy pulled out her chair and sat down. Her mother slid a floppy omelette onto her plate. Bits of melted cheese oozed around it. Lucy wasn't hungry, but she knew she was going to have to sit through this dinner anyway.

"I think a bit of white wine would go down very well," said her mother. "Would you like a taste?"

"No thanks," said Lucy.

Both her parents were crazy about wine and they talked about it a lot. Sometimes when they opened a special wine with dinner, Lucy got a little lecture about it. They would pour a tiny bit for her, and she was supposed to taste it, and make some sort of comment about it. As far as Lucy was concerned, it all tasted pretty awful. Then she would get those funny grown-up smiles from her parents, and she would feel shut out — almost as though both of them had their own private world, and she was just an amusing toy.

Her mother poured herself a glass of wine, raised her glass and said, *"Bon appétit."*

Lucy cut her omelette into little squares and pushed them around with her fork. Her salad bowl stayed untouched by her side. Her mother cheerfully dug into the food. Every now and then she would have a small sip of wine.

"You're not eating, Lucy."

Lucy looked up from her plate, where a small pyramid of omelette slivers waited, untouched.

"I'm not that hungry, Mom."

"What's the matter? Don't tell me you've stuffed yourself with that carrot cake!"

"I don't feel that great... I'm just not very hungry."

The excuse sounded lame even to Lucy.

"I hope you're not coming down with something." Her mom leaned forward and touched Lucy's forehead. "Hmm, you do feel a little warm."

"Mom," said Lucy, pushing herself away from the table, "I hope you don't mind, but I just want to go upstairs and lie down."

"Okay Lucy. An early night will be good for you, especially since none of you will sleep this weekend."

Lucy picked up her dinner plate and put it in the kitchen sink.

If only her mother knew what was happening on the weekend! She walked up to her room, and changed into her nightgown. Lying on her bed, Lucy actually felt a little sick. All I need, is to really come down with something, she thought miserably. When did the travel agency open in the morning? She would have to get out of first period to telephone. There was no point in calling anyone now.

Just before Lucy turned off her light, her mother came into her room and felt her forehead again.

"Good. I don't think you have a temperature."

"I'll be fine. I'm going to sleep, Mom." Lucy avoided her mother's eyes.

It wasn't that easy. Lucy tossed and turned for hours. The trick was to clear your mind, just like switching off the television. What's happened to my remote control, thought Lucy. Why doesn't it clear the screen? Just when she would stop thinking about one thing, another thought would pop up. She kept seeing herself waiting for a ride to the airport — while Clutch, with the blonde girl beside him, sat in his car with "Mr. Action" painted on the Clutchmobile.

Then she'd see herself at the airport, and somebody in a uniform was asking for her passport. L.D.'s warnings echoed in her head. It was like being on a carousel which never stopped. There had to be a way around it. She had to find that way, or her fantasy vacation would come tumbling down. If that happened, how on earth would she face her friends or her parents? It was a horrible thought, and one that stayed with her until she fell asleep.

CHAPTER 13

Lucy woke up the next morning to find her mother leaning over her.

"How are you feeling Lucy?"

"I'm fine," said Lucy in a sleepy, fuzzy voice.

"Don't forget to have breakfast," said her mom, patting her face and walking away.

Lucy got out of bed and headed for the bathroom. She didn't want to waste any time at home this morning. There was a big problem waiting to be solved.

When she got to school, she saw L.D., Erica and Heather sitting on the steps waiting for her. They had apprehensive looks on their faces, and Lucy felt her heart sink a little. Obviously, they had been discussing her. L.D. must have told them about last night's conversation.

"Hi Lucy," chorused the twins.

L.D. just gave her a worried look.

"It's okay, I'm going to call the travel agency at nine," said Lucy.

"I don't think places like that open till ten," chirped Heather.

"I'll try anyway," replied Lucy briskly.

All four of them walked towards their lockers in silence. There were posters stuck everywhere on the school walls. The posters were part of a pre-graduation campaign asking for volunteers and suggestions. Lucy barely noticed them. She was a million miles away. It was ten to nine. She had ten minutes to go before she found out what her fate would be.

First period was Mr. Raditch's class. The minute he walked in, everybody in the class settled down. Lucy waited for five minutes before she put her hand up.

"May I be excused for a minute?" she asked.

Mr. Raditch looked at Lucy and nodded. Lucy got up and moved towards the door. Over her shoulder she saw L.D. move her lips silently. L.D. crossed the fingers of both hands and raised them up so Lucy could see them. Yes, thought Lucy to herself, I need all the luck in the world right now.

Lucy looked up and down the corridor. The

only telephone the students at Degrassi Junior High could use was in the office. You had to go up to Doris and tell her why the call had to be made. Then when you made the call, Doris sat close by pretending not to hear. Everybody knew that she heard everything anyway. Lucy couldn't use that phone. The other phone was in the staff room. Heading towards the staff room, Lucy prayed that it was empty. It was first period, and all the teachers should be in class.

Lucy opened the door very gently. It was empty! She dashed up to the phone which sat on a little table. It was five minutes past nine. She dialed the number of the travel agency with shaky fingers. It rang five times, and then it was picked up.

"Vacation Paradise, good morning," sang the voice on the other end.

"I would like some information please," said Lucy.

"How can I help you?"

"Do you need a passport to travel to the Bahamas?"

"Not if you are a Canadian citizen," answered the travel agent. "But you do need identification. A driver's license or birth certificate will do."

"Thank you, thank you so much!" Lucy squeaked into the phone.

She slammed the phone down and twirled around in the staff room. It was all over — all the insane worry and the heart-sick feeling of defeat — tomorrow she would be off, just the way she had planned. She felt like running down the corridor singing and shouting. But first, she had to get out of the staff room before anyone saw her.

Lucy stuck her head out of the staff room door and looked down the corridor. It was empty. She skipped and jogged back to class. Mr. Raditch was standing at the blackboard. Three pairs of anxious eyes followed Lucy back to her seat. Lucy pasted the biggest happiest smile on her face and made a thumbs up sign to L.D.

When first period was over the twins and L.D. pounced on her.

"What, what, what?" chanted Erica.

"I don't need a passport," whispered Lucy.

"I'm so glad, Lucy. We were *so* worried!" Heather squeezed Lucy's arm.

"I knew it," chortled Erica. "Your horoscope said you would overcome a big obstacle."

"Oh, you're such a nit, Erica!" exploded L.D. "Something could still happen."

"What do you mean?" said Lucy indignantly.

"You still have tomorrow."

123

"L.D. everything is going to be just fine."

Lucy felt giddy, swept up by an excitement which coloured everything. She felt alive and fearless. Later that afternoon she told L.D. and the twins how Clutch had wanted to come with her. She hadn't planned on telling them but it just tumbled out. L.D. just rolled her eyes at this new piece of information.

Erica tossed her curls. "Why not? I think it would be neat to run away with someone as cute as Clutch."

"Yeah, and wind up sleeping in the same room with him," said Heather in a sarcastic tone.

"I'm sleeping in a room by myself with tropical breezes," giggled Lucy.

"Lucy, I just don't know about Clutch. I'm really worried about him for tomorrow," said L.D.

Lucy ignored L.D.'s comment. There was no point in saying anything. She was going to worry herself to death over Clutch. That was the only negative thing about L.D., and she was used to it. Everything else about L.D. was so terrific. She was the best friend anyone could ever have.

"Who's coming to the airport with us?" she asked, looking at all three of them.

"We can't make it. I don't think it's a good idea," said Heather firmly.

"I'll go with you," said L.D.

"I really wanted to come Lucy, but...." Erica shrugged her shoulders apologetically.

"It's okay," said Lucy quickly. She didn't want to cause any trouble between Erica and Heather. They were willing to stick their necks out for her, and that's what counted. What neither of them knew was that her mother would never call their house. After school, when Lucy was walking home, L.D. pressed a small envelope into her hands. There were thirty dollars inside.

"Thanks, L.D. I'll pay it back," promised Lucy.

"It's okay," L.D. started laughing.

"What's so funny?" demanded Lucy.

L.D. laughed her head off for a minute and finally she gasped, "I was going to say, and don't skip town!"

Lucy laughed along with her. She was going to skip town, but she would make sure she repaid L.D. With the fifty dollars that her mom had given her the total came to eighty. Her meals were paid for, so it was basically spending money. She would buy presents for the three of them and hang on to the rest for anything else that came up.

After saying goodbye to L.D., Lucy raced home. She had to call Clutch and make sure that he was still going to give her the ride to the airport. She didn't want him to park right outside the main entrance. After all she was going to be cutting school, and it wouldn't be a good idea to be seen leaving. If they bumped into a teacher there would be all sorts of questions.

Clutch picked up his phone on the first ring. "Hi," he said.

"Clutch… " started Lucy, feeling a little apprehensive.

"So tomorrow is the big day." He sounded okay.

"Yes," replied Lucy. At least he wasn't being unfriendly.

"All packed?"

"Are you still going to drive?"

There was a small pause, and Lucy's heart sank.

"Sure."

"Oh, thank you," Lucy gasped in relief. Then she added, "Clutch, we have to take off from school without anyone seeing us."

"Don't worry, I'll take care of it. I may even have a surprise for you."

"A surprise?"

"Yeah, something you can take along with you."

"Oh… I can hardly wait," said Lucy. Clutch was all right. Well, better to say it all now. "Clutch, I think you'd better be prepared. L.D. is going to come along as well."

There was a pause. What is it with both of them, thought Lucy. They don't even know each other, but they dislike each other.

"Figures," said Clutch finally.

"Clutch, she's my best friend. I couldn't have done this without her help."

"It's all right. It's just that she isn't exactly a ball of sunshine."

"She's terrific," said Lucy firmly.

"Sure," said Clutch. He didn't sound convinced. "Well, see you tomorrow."

"Thanks, Clutch," said Lucy. She really meant it.

"Hey, no problem."

The evening flew by. Lucy checked the contents of her handbag. She tucked the money deep in her billfold. The birth certificate and the sunglasses were slipped into the zippered section. Lucy filled two small plastic bottles with shampoo and conditioner and tossed them into the duffle bag. She would change at school tomorrow. L.D. would take her school stuff and her jacket home with her. There was no way she could take her winter jacket with her to the Bahamas. The last thing Lucy had to do was write a fake letter from her mother saying she would be away on Monday.

Finally everything was done. Lucy went to the kitchen to find something to eat. There was a note from her mother on the kitchen table. She was to put a casserole in the oven for dinner. Lucy jerked the fridge door open, took the casserole out and slammed the door shut. One of these days she was going to tell her mother that eating alone was the most horrible thing in the world. This was the time when she really felt abandoned. She would never get used to it. The empty house ached for sound. She switched the television on. Her mother was going to be late again, and the television would keep her company. That's how it worked for now, but tomorrow everything would be different. She wasn't going to be plain, old Lucy Fernandez who was growing up alone because her parents were too busy for her. She was going to be a carefree, glamourous traveller.

CHAPTER 14

When Lucy woke up on Friday morning, she knew that something was happening outside. She looked out her window. The entire street was white. Snowflakes spun around merrily and driveways were being shovelled. After two weeks of a freezing, but dry February, finally a snowfall! There would be a mad snowball fight at Degrassi, and some of the younger kids would end up at the office complaining.

When Lucy turned away from the window, the first thing that caught her eye was her wall calendar — FRIDAY with its red pen circles bounced off the calendar — and a shiver of excitement rippled through her. It had finally arrived. No more waiting and planning, thought Lucy. It's happening to me today. I'm off, and when every one else gets home in the evening to shovel more snow, I'll be sitting on a beach.

Her alarm clock told her that she had exactly one hour to get ready. Lucy had a shower, got dressed and pulled the duffle bag out from under her bed. She checked downstairs. There was no sign of her mother, so she carried everything down to the kitchen. She pulled out a large green garbage bag and put her duffle bag inside it. It would look funny, but she didn't want it getting wet in the snow. Besides, this way no one would know what it was. Lucy gulped down a muffin and a glass of orange juice in record speed. Then she ran upstairs.

Lucy hesitated outside her mother's room. She was torn — part of her wanted to just walk away, but another part of her wanted to say goodbye. Lucy pushed the door open and walked in to her mom's bedroom. Her mother turned her head and slowly opened her eyes.

"Lucy, what time is it?"

"It's almost eight. I've got to go, Mom." Lucy knew her mother was still half asleep.

"Mmmmm," murmured her mom. She pushed herself up. "I didn't hear the alarm."

"It's snowing, Mom. I have to go. I don't want to be late."

"Have you had breakfast?" Her mom was

sitting up now.

"Yes. Bye, Mom… and see you on Monday night."

"Monday night?"

"Yeah… it's Friday. I'm spending the weekend with the twins, remember? I won't be back till Monday night." Better get this straight, Lucy thought.

"Goodness! Is it Friday?" Her mother gave a big yawn. "Yes, yes, of course. Lucy, be a good weekend guest, please."

"Sure, and say 'hi' to Dad for me. I've got to go, Mom."

"Lucy," said her mother, halting Lucy's dash to the door.

"Yeah… what?"

"Is there a lot of snow?"

"I think so."

"That's all we need," shuddered her mother. She closed her eyes and flopped down on the bed again.

Lucy went to her room for a last minute check. She hadn't left anything behind. She went down and pulled out her winter boots from the front hall closet. Slinging her hand bag over one arm, and lifting the garbage bag with the other, she let herself out of the front door.

The walk to school normally took her eight minutes. Today she had to walk more slowly.

The pavements were slippery and the garbage bag kept slipping out of her fingers. By the time she reached Degrassi it was torn. The snow kept falling, and because her hands were full she couldn't even put the hood of her jacket up. Her hair was wet and she felt cold all over.

Snowball fights had already begun in the front yard of the school. As Lucy struggled up the steps, somebody threw a snowball which caught her on the side of the face. Stunned and furious, Lucy dropped the garbage bag and turned around, but the kids had turned away and it was hard to tell who had done it.

Lucy lifted the garbage bag and moved towards the entrance door. Footsteps behind her made her turn. It was L.D. Her jacket hood was pulled up snug around her face.

"Hi L.D.," said Lucy. "Did you see the little brats with the snowballs? I could just kill them."

"Yes. You could, couldn't you?" L.D. snapped.

Lucy swung around in astonishment and looked at L.D. "What's your problem?" she asked.

L.D. shouldered Lucy aside. "Move this junk. I want to get inside," she muttered.

Startled, Lucy watched L.D. jerk open the

door and fling herself inside without looking back.

Junk, thought Lucy, looking at her ripped garbage bag. The duffle bag was spilling out. Then she looked at L.D.'s fast-moving back. Something was wrong. L.D. had acted as though Lucy was her enemy instead of her best friend. It was cold outside, but the expression on L.D.'s face was colder.

Dragging the garbage bag, Lucy headed towards the girls' washroom. As she walked in, she almost stumbled into L.D., who was walking out.

"Watch where you're going," hissed L.D. at her.

"What is wrong with you?" Lucy stammered in shock.

"Get out of my way, Lucy!"

"Just a minute." Lucy grabbed L.D.'s arm. "Why are you being so awful to me?"

"You want to know? Well, I'm just dying to tell you." L.D. wrenched her arm away from Lucy. L.D.'s eyes were the eyes of a cold stranger. Something about her expression made Lucy brace herself.

"Well?" she said.

"They caught the people who robbed my dad's garage last night."

"What's that got to do with me? I didn't rob your dad's garage!"

"Guess who they were, Lucy?" said L.D. Her voice was sinister.

"I don't know! This has nothing to do with me!" L.D.'s anger frightened her.

"They were a bunch of high school kids. And do you want to know whose car they driving that night?"

"You tell me," replied Lucy. L.D. had really gone crazy.

"It was the *Clutchmobile*."

Lucy felt as though she had been drenched with a bucket of icy water. She gasped with shock and backed away from L.D. It couldn't be true.

"You want to know something else, Lucy?" L.D advanced towards her. "My father was giving me this lecture about kids and dishonesty, and committing crimes, and I wanted to throw up, because I couldn't tell him my best friend knows the owner of the car."

"L.D., just because Clutch lent his car to someone doesn't mean he did it," blurted Lucy desperately.

"I know exactly why you're defending him," retaliated L.D. furiously.

"No, you don't. You're accusing him for no reason. You're ruining everything."

"You know what, Lucy? You're just like him. Clutch lends his car to people who steal, and you steal all by yourself. I don't want to have anything to do with you!"

"So you're going to let me down is that it?" asked Lucy.

L.D didn't reply. Lucy looked at L.D. and her heart sank. The unthinkable had happened. Her best friend was going to abandon her. Well, she'd show her. She'd show all of them that she didn't care.

"Are you going to squeal on me, L.D.?" asked Lucy. Her voice was dangerously soft.

"What do you think I am?"

"I'll tell you what I think," said Lucy, recklessly. "I think you've always hated Clutch. Even if he didn't know what his friends did with his car, you'd still accuse him. I think you're jealous of me. And you're no friend of mine!"

L.D. turned her face away abruptly and walked out. Lucy brushed furiously at the angry tears spilling down her face. With shaking hands she removed the duffle bag from the garbage bag and walked out of the washroom towards her locker. Erica and Heather were waiting for her.

"I can't believe it, Lucy. I can't believe it's today." Erica gave Lucy a hug.

"Neither can I," said Lucy.

"Will it fit?" said Heather. She struggled to fit the duffle bag in her locker.

"It just has to," muttered Lucy. She crammed the duffle bag into the locker and slammed the door.

"Have you seen what's happening out-side?" said Heather.

"Who cares?" said Lucy wearily. She headed for class. Erica and Heather followed, exchanging puzzled looks. By lunchtime, everybody in class knew that something was happening between L.D. and Lucy. L.D. refused to look at Lucy. Erica and Heather kept whispering to both of them. Even the teacher commented that too much talking was going on. Lucy found herself avoiding L.D.'s desk and wondering whether the police had impounded Clutch's car if it had been used in a robbery. She was right in the middle of the biggest mess, and there was no way she could think it away. The only thing she knew was that nothing that L.D. said would stop her from going on the trip.

When it was time for lunch and they dashed off to the lunch room, Lucy realized that she had forgotten to pack a lunch. L.D. was missing. Erica shoved half her lunch at Lucy.

"Where's L.D.?" she asked. "What's going on?"

"I don't know, and I don't care," said Lucy.

"Don't tell me. You've had a fight!" Erica

136

looked horrified.

"Something like that," mumbled Lucy wretchedly.

"But she's your best friend," exclaimed Heather.

"Not anymore. Look, I don't want to talk about it, okay?"

"We're still your friends," piped up Erica, giving Heather an imploring look.

"Of course we are," said Heather promptly.

"Lucy, do you want me to come with you to the airport?" offered Erica.

"It's okay, I'll be fine. Clutch is going to be there, and he and L.D. never did get along."

"Are you sure?"

"Yeah, I'm sure."

When first period after lunch ended, Lucy and the twins walked to the lockers together. They collected Lucy's bag and went in to the girls' washroom.

"Bye, Lucy," said Erica. She gave Lucy a big hug. "Have a blast."

"I hope you have a great time, and please, be careful," whispered Heather.

"I will," said Lucy, putting her arms around Heather.

"Well, we better get to class," said Erica reluctantly.

The twins waved goodbye and walked out.

Lucy wiggled out of her jeans and pulled her travelling outfit from the duffle bag. She slipped into the long skirt and top and pulled her jacket over it.

"This is crazy," muttered Lucy, not liking what she saw in the mirror. Why did the outfit make her look so dowdy? Reluctantly she zipped up the duffle bag, and without looking at the mirror again she walked out into the corridor. Keeping one eye peeled for teachers, she walked quickly towards the back exit.

Lucy shivered as she stepped out the door. She was wearing summer clothes under her winter jacket, and her legs were cold. The duffle bag felt heavy. Looking down the street, Lucy couldn't see the Clutchmobile, but there was a figure waiting halfway down the street. Lucy quickened her steps. He's probably parked it around the corner, she thought — good old Clutch. As she got closer, Lucy realized that the person was wearing a straw hat. Was it the snowflakes half blinding her? The person turned towards her. It was Clutch, and he was wearing a wide-brimmed, straw hat and the biggest smile in the world.

Lucy ran up to him.

"Here I am," said Lucy.

"At your service, babe." Clutch tilted the

brim of his hat. "All the way."

"You're crazy," giggled Lucy. She felt better already. "Is that your airport driving hat?"

"Nope... it's my standard holiday gear." Clutch grabbed the duffle from Lucy.

"What do you mean?" said Lucy.

"I'm coming with you to the Bahamas... I thought I'd surprise you." He put his hand on his heart and spoke theatrically. "Can't do without you, you know. Not for one minute."

"What's going on, Clutch?" Lucy couldn't believe what she had just heard.

"Relax, I checked up. There are lots of tickets on your flight. My friend Paul has his father's pick-up, and he's waiting around the corner to drive us." Clutch put his free arm around Lucy's waist.

"Clutch, why are you doing this?"

"Come on, let's go," Clutch said, ignoring Lucy's question.

Lucy pushed Clutch's arm away, hysteria rising within her.

"I'm not going with you, Clutch. I thought you knew that."

"Hey, we'll have an absolute blast," protested Clutch.

"Oh, God," wailed Lucy, "L.D. was right about you. How am I going to get to the airport?"

"Paul's going to drive us. Come on, we're going to be late."

"You're a real jerk, Clutch," shouted Lucy. "I'm not going anywhere with you — or your friends."

"Aw, come on Lucy." Clutch sounded annoyed. "What's your problem? You want to have a good time — so do I. We'll be great together."

"Give me my bag," screamed Lucy.

They stood there for a moment tugging at the duffle bag, sliding in the softly falling snow. Lucy was panting with shock and anger. She couldn't believe this was happening.

"I hate you!" she yelled at Clutch, giving one savage tug, she loosened the bag from Clutch's grip. "Don't you dare follow me. I *never* want to see you again!"

"What are you going to do?" shouted Clutch.

"I'm going to take the bus."

"Chicken!" sneered Clutch.

Lucy ran awkwardly towards the corner bus stop. Miraculously, as she reached it, a bus pulled up. Lucy stepped into the bus without looking back. She was soaked, and the zipper on the duffle bag was sliding open. She had just over a hour and a half to get to the airport.

First L.D., and then Clutch — both of them had let her down in the worst possible way. She would never forgive them. Now she was really alone.

CHAPTER 15

Lucy stared out of the bus window in a daze. Nothing made sense anymore. Here she was on her way to the airport, at the start of her big adventure — but instead of the good feelings she had anticipated, she felt abandoned and lonely. It was L.D. and Clutch who were responsible for all this. What was going to happen to her if she couldn't rely on her parents or her friends? Getting away was the only answer.

The airport bus was half full. Lucy looked at all the adults around her and shrank closer to the wall next to her seat. She was convinced that she looked like a fool. The hem of her skirt was wet and her ski jacket felt sloppy. She was supposed to send the jacket back with L.D. I hate you L.D., Lucy thought to herself. You're supposed to be my friend, and instead you made me feel as though I was personally responsible for your father's robbery.

Suddenly, Clutch's face swam before her — laughing, flirtatious Clutch, whom she didn't know at all. When he yelled "chicken" at her, the contours of his face had changed. He's a rule-breaker, thought Lucy, and so am I — that's why, we're attracted to each other — that's all it is.

Lucy glanced at her watch. It was 2:45. She didn't even know how long the bus would take to get to the airport. Her flight left at four.

Seated across the aisle from her was a couple. They held each other's hand. The woman talked excitedly and then the man leaned over and kissed her. They were so preoccupied with each other that it didn't matter who was looking at them. Lucy kept stealing glances at them. She was drawn to the romantic air that hovered around them. It also made her forget that she was alone. Maybe they would end up on the same trip with her.

As the bus sped along the highway, Lucy pulled out her cosmetics kit and decided to put on some make-up. Her clothes might look awful, but at least she would have a perfect face.

"You're so pretty, you don't need all that," said a female voice.

Lucy looked up. It was the woman seated across the aisle. She had leaned forward to look at Lucy and was smiling at her. Lucy felt so embarrassed that she instantly snapped her make-up pouch shut.

"I hope you don't mind my saying that," continued the woman.

"No... it's okay," stammered Lucy.

"Are you off on a trip somewhere?" asked the woman.

"Yes, I am," said Lucy.

"Where are you going?"

"To the Bahamas."

"Oh, you lucky person. We're going back to Calgary."

Lucy noticed the gleam of excitement in the woman's eyes, and found it reassuring. Here was an adult, someone she didn't even know, who was excited for her. She had done the best thing after all.

"Are you meeting your family at the airport?" went on the woman.

"No, I'm travelling alone," replied Lucy softly.

"Oh! What fun!"

Lucy drew back in her seat a little. She knew the woman was just being friendly, but she wasn't ready for questions. It could get

144

dangerous. After all the disasters, she didn't want anything else to happen. She glanced at her watch and looked out at the airport signs which were beginning to appear on the highway. It was almost three, but they were getting closer to the airport.

"Well, have a good trip." The woman gave her a little wave and settled back in her seat.

She's a little like Mom, thought Lucy. She thought about her mother. Would she call the twins' house? Probably not. She would be too busy selling houses to even think of Lucy.

I'm growing up on my own because they don't care about me, thought Lucy. She knew she wouldn't get into too much trouble when she got home. Especially if she came back looking terrific and happy. Her father had said to her once, "All we want is for you to be happy." Well, she had decided to make herself happy.

The bus moved up a ramp, and the airport terminal appeared. She had arrived. She had forty-nine minutes left to catch the flight. Lucy bounded up from her seat. The bus stopped and a flurry of activity started around her. The passengers pulled down their hand baggage. There were lots of business men with briefcases. Lucy slung her handbag over her shoulder and moved towards the front of the bus.

The bus driver was outside removing luggage from the bus. Lucy waited for her bag. It took awhile. When the bus driver handed the duffle bag to her, he smiled. "This one looks like it's going around the world," he said.

Lucy smiled back. She lifted the duffle bag and turned towards the big, glass-plate doors. She had walked up to the first one, before she realized it was the "out" door. Lucy looked over her shoulder to see if anyone had seen her make such a silly mistake, but people just milled around without looking at anything. Right next to it was the "in" door. Lucy walked through.

The terminal was an absolute zoo. Nothing had prepared Lucy for the sight before her. There were hundreds of people with tons of luggage littered all over the place. Each counter had a line-up of about fifteen or twenty people. All sorts of announcements were being made, but you couldn't even make out the words. Lucy looked around helplessly. She didn't even know where her ticket counter was. How was she going to get up to the top of the line-ups and find out? How much time was it going to take?

Lucy tried to look around for somebody who she could ask. She could feel a sense of panic welling up inside. It was that old, sick feeling of nervousness — wanting to do something and not knowing how to take the first step. She tried to walk in between the lines and read the signs above the counters. There were flight numbers and destinations and then names of tours everywhere. Everybody seemed to be irritable or too busy. Lucy tripped over luggage and lines of grim faced people as she moved along the width of the terminal.

I've got to find the Vacation Paradise people, she thought desperately. She paused in front of a line-up and turned to a man who was standing at the end.

"Excuse me, can you tell me how to find — I mean — where the flights go to the Bahamas?"

The man gave Lucy a disinterested look. "Flights to the Caribbean are over there," he said. He jerked his thumb toward the other end of the terminal.

Lucy looked down to where he was pointing. She had just come from that end. She looked at her watch. It said 3:20. Turning around, she started fighting her way through the crowds again. When she reached the end of the terminal, she saw a long line-up of people. Some of them were wearing straw hats.

Lucy kept murmuring "excuse me" and

tried to get to the counter so she could see
the sign. It was the right counter all right.
Her flight number and destination was
posted on the sign behind the counter. There
were two ticket agents busy handling tickets,
and even though Lucy tried to catch their
eye, it just didn't work. They looked right
through her.

Lucy walked back to the end of the line.
She put her duffle bag down in front of her.
The line would inch up slowly to the counter,
and she would just have to wait her turn.
Please let this line move fast, prayed Lucy
silently. Why had she ever thought going to
the airport was fun? In ten minutes she had
become as irritable and grim-faced as
everyone around her. She felt and looked
grubby. The only consolation was that at
least there was no one around to see her in
this condition.

Lucy shuffled from one foot to the other. A
young man wearing a maple-leaf T-shirt was
standing in front of her. Taking a deep
breath, she spoke to him. "What happens if
you don't make it to the counter in time?"

The young man scratched his beard and
looked at her. "Don't worry, we're all in the
same boat," he said.

"Yes, but don't you have to check in a hour
before your flight?" Lucy asked. She could

hear the agitation in her voice.

"Relax," drawled the young man, "nobody is going to fly the plane before we're all in... Going to Nassau?"

"No, I am going to the Bahamas," said Lucy.

"Oh yeah," said the man. He gave her a peculiar smile. "Well, I guess I'll see you there."

No, you won't, Lucy said to herself. You sound like a real creep, and I don't want to be anywhere near you. I don't even know, thought Lucy, whether I want to be here. All of a sudden she thought of everyone at school. What were they doing right now? L.D. would still be mad at her. Would she talk to Erica and Heather, get them confused, maybe even get them thinking like L.D.? Lucy imagined all of them gossiping about her as they walked home, without knowing how absolutely miserable she felt at this moment. This day, thought Lucy, has been full of nasty surprises.

CHAPTER 16

There were only three people ahead of Lucy. She kicked her duffle bag forward, and stepped up right behind it. The creepy guy wearing the maple-leaf T-shirt turned around. "Almost there," he said. Lucy drew back from him. Something about the way he looked at her made her uncomfortable. His eyes slithered all over her body when he talked, and the effect was as unpleasant as having an ant crawling on you. It would be awful if she wound up sitting next to him.

The people at the counter moved away, and the creepy guy moved up to the counter. Lucy was right behind him. She bent down to pick up her duffle bag. As she straightened up, a hand grabbed her shoulder.

"Lucy, what are you doing here?" said a voice behind her.

Lucy froze. She felt as though she was in the middle of a great explosion — but she was rooted — unable to move. She knew the voice very well.

"What is going on?" The hand turned her around, forcefully.

Lucy looked into her father's eyes, and almost fainted. He stood there holding a travelling case and shoulder bag. He had a shocked look on his face, and his eyes were confused.

What are you doing here, Lucy wanted to scream, you're not supposed to be back until tomorrow — but terror kept her mouth sealed. She knew it was all over. There would be an empty seat on that plane going to the Bahamas. She stepped out of the line and tried to open her mouth again, to say something, but all she did was swallow air a few times.

"Why aren't you in school? What's in this bag?" Her father was recovering. He sounded angry.

Lucy knew that people around them were listening. She looked down at her feet, wanting to disappear, to melt away like a blob. Tears started pushing at her eyelids and she knew that it would be just a matter of seconds before they rolled down her face.

"Come here," said her father, beckoning to

her. He moved away from the line-up, "I want an explanation of all this, and I want it fast. My God, if I hadn't come down here to clear up my car rental mix-up, I never would have seen you!"

Lucy followed him, the tears half-blinding her. Her father pushed his way through the crowd to the back of the terminal near the glass-plate doors. He propped his bags on the metal ledge by the window, plucked the duffle bag from her hands, and tossed it on the pile of baggage.

"Now," he said, planting both hands on his hips, "I want to know what's going on?"

"I was going on a trip, Daddy," sobbed Lucy, unable to control herself.

"Does your mother know about this?"

"No."

"I see. Where were you going?"

"I had booked one of those vacation packages. " Lucy spoke very slowly.

"*What*?!" Her father yelled so loudly that people around them actually stopped. His face turned red with anger. He was silent for a moment, and Lucy could feel he was trying to control himself.

"Running away, Lucy?" He spoke carefully.

"I was fed up. I was going to take off for a few days... just for the weekend," babbled

Lucy.

"I see," said her father. His voice was dangerously soft. "Who is paying for this trip?"

Lucy felt more tears beginning to roll down her face. They had reached the awful part, and nothing would get her out of this one. In the tiniest imaginable voice she said, "I charged it on Mom's Visa." She could see the shock register on her father's face. He drew back as though he had been punched.

"Where is the ticket?" he said, holding out his hand.

"I had to pick it up at the counter," replied Lucy, avoiding her father's eyes.

"Stay here... *and don't move*," yelled her father furiously.

Lucy watched him walk towards the ticket counters. He's going to kill me, thought Lucy. She looked around her desperately. People continued to walk in and out. Nobody was interested in Lucy Fernandez, dressed in her mother's skirt and a sloppy ski jacket, huddled in the corner. It was face the medicine time. She had to do it all alone this time. L.D.'s words were coming back to haunt her. What a fool she had been. For the first time since the beginning of the horrible day, she knew that L.D. was not a worry wart. The ugly scene that morning had occurred because L.D. had been really offended. She had behaved just like Clutch. She hadn't cared about anyone but herself. When she saw her father returning, Lucy could feel herself shrinking towards the pile of luggage behind her. As he came closer, she saw that he had a different expression on his face.

"Well, I've told them that the card was stolen by my daughter," said her father, looking wearily at her.

The word "stolen" pierced Lucy like an arrow. Even though her father had said it in a matter-of-fact voice, the impact on Lucy was shattering. It was a humiliating word, carrying its own dark shadow with it. Even if you moved, the shadow stayed with you. This word, will smother me, thought Lucy.

"Daddy, I'm sorry," she whispered to her father.

"So am I, Lucy," said her father. He shook his head and looked away from her into the distance.

"I won't ever — "

Her father silenced her with a gesture. "I want to call your mother."

Lucy watched him search his pockets for some change and turn to the phones close by.

"Please don't call mom," Lucy pleaded.

Her father ignored her, dialing the phone with jerky fingers.

"I want to tell her myself, later," cried Lucy, her voice high-pitched with fear.

Luck was on her side. No one picked up the phone.

"Hardly the message to leave on the answering machine," said her father in a grim voice.

Lucy knew it would be easier once she got home. Home now meant something different. It was a place where you could hide. Standing here at the airport she felt exposed. It felt as though the entire airport knew that Lucy Fernandez had stolen her mother's Visa card.

"I'm exhausted, I've been travelling all day Lucy, and now *this*!"

"I'm sorry, I'm so sorry," repeated Lucy.

"Well, let's get out of here, I have to collect the car," said her father shortly.

Maybe it's over, thought Lucy hopefully, maybe, I'll get a lecture on the way home, and Mom will do the same. Then I can jump into my bed and pull the covers up and just sleep all this away. She followed her father into the elevator which took them up to the parking lot. The elevator ride was a silent one. There were other people in the car, and thankfully her dad didn't say anything. He didn't even look at her. He's wishing he didn't have a daughter like me, Lucy thought miserably.

It took awhile to find her dad's car. When he tossed the bags in the back seat, and opened the door for her, Lucy braced herself. Here it comes, she thought. Now he's going to tell me how awful I am and then there will be a punishment of some sort — maybe she'd be grounded, or her allowance docked.

But her father pulled out of the parking lot silently. The car pulled up on the highway, and the silence in the car was the only alive thing around. Her father kept his face ahead looking out at the road. Lucy kept stealing glances at him, thinking any minute he would say something, but he didn't.

Lucy could feel her palms sweating, and a sick kind of tension jumped and quivered through her entire body. She knew if she didn't say something she would burst.

"Daddy," she said for the fifth time, "I *am* sorry, I won't do it again."

Her father didn't even acknowledge what she had said. He kept quiet for awhile, and then he turned sideways and gave Lucy a furious look.

"This is a serious problem, Lucy. I don't even know you anymore."

"It was just meant to be... a wild kind of thing to do — you know, like an adventure... something I'd never done before," jumped in

Lucy.

"An *adventure*!" snorted her father. "No, Lucy, you've got it all wrong."

Lucy had never heard her father sound like that — angry, tired, and sort of defeated. She'd done that. She had made him feel like this. Part of her felt terrible, but she realized that another part of her was secretly pleased. At least she had his attention. For a moment, it felt like a small victory. After all, she had been feeling lost and defeated for a long time. It wasn't just her mom who was never home. For her dad, too, his job always seemed to come first. She wanted to tell him that. She wanted to scream it out loud, loud enough to shatter the silence and make him understand. His voice broke in on her thoughts.

"I've been thinking, Lucy, very hard and very furiously but I'm going to save it until we get home. Then we can have this out with your mom there too."

"I don't think I can face Mom," Lucy blurted out.

"You're going to Lucy. She's going to be very interested to find out what is happening to her daughter," replied her father firmly.

That's what you think, thought Lucy.

CHAPTER 17

The car pulled into the driveway and rolled to a stop. Lucy fought the impulse to leap out of the car and run. The last thing she wanted to do was to walk in through the front door. She tried to think desperately of a way out. Her father came around to her side and opened her door, and the small gust of cold wind that blew in chilled Lucy to the bone.

"Let's go, Lucy," he said.

Lucy stumbled out of the car. She threw her father a last beseeching look, but he motioned her towards the door.

Before her dad had a chance to fumble with the door handle, it swung open. Her mother stood in the entrance. Lucy put her head down and slunk in behind her dad. Her mother looked at her and her eyes widened.

"Where did you meet Daddy?"

"We bumped into each other," said her father, not prepared to help.

"Aren't you supposed to be at the twins'?" asked her mother.

Lucy took a deep breath and then exhaled sharply. This was the moment. It had finally arrived. She gave one last look at her father, who walked past her into the living room. He settled into a chair and loosened his tie.

"What is happening here?" said her mother in a sharp voice, looking from Mr. Fernandez to Lucy.

You're on your own, said a voice inside Lucy.

"I bumped into Daddy at the airport," said Lucy in a quavering voice.

"At the *airport*!" repeated her mother. "What were you doing there... and why are you wearing my clothes?"

Lucy felt as though a rock was stuck in her throat. She looked down at her hands in misery. They had curled themselves involuntarily — tense, tight, little balls of palms and fingers. The rest of her body braced itself for the attack. She knew it was coming.

"I'm talking to you Lucy," said her mother sharply.

"I...I was going to take a trip." Lucy kept staring at her hands. Her voice was low.

159

"You were what?"

"I was going to take a trip... to the Bahamas."

"Lucy, I...." Her mother shook her head. "Do you mean to tell me that if your father hadn't seen you at the airport, you'd be on a plane to the Bahamas right now?"

Lucy nodded.

"And when were you planning to come back? Or were you?"

"Monday," said Lucy. "It was a three-day package."

"I can't believe this," whispered her mother with a pale, expressionless face. "I can't believe that my fifteen-year-old daughter was going to go the Bahamas for the weekend."

Lucy nodded dumbly.

"All these stories about you going to the twins', and the birthday party, and the presents!" She stopped, and her eyes narrowed. "Just how did you pay for this trip?"

Lucy squeezed her hands together until they hurt. She looked up at her mother. "I charged it on your Visa."

Her mother gasped, "Lucy."

"I'm sorry," started Lucy.

"Be quiet," interrupted her mother fiercely, "you've been lying to me for days, haven't you?"

She began to pace up and down the room, and stopped in front of Lucy.

"What else have you charged on my Visa?"

"Nothing else."

"Do you expect me to believe you?" shouted her mother indignantly.

"Please Mom, I want you to believe me now," pleaded Lucy.

"It means checking up on you Lucy, all over the place."

"You can check, Mom... I promise... I just got the ticket on it."

"Did it ever occur to you," said her father, jerking off his tie angrily, "that all this energy, this fine planning, could have gone into something good?"

"It was just meant to be an adventure." said Lucy.

"*Adventure!*" yelled her father, "No, Lucy, you've really got it all wrong! Adventures do not mean you cheat and lie and steal."

Her mother did not say a word. She just stood there with her arms folded across her chest with a grim expression on her face. Lucy felt tears rising in her eyes again. She knew her parents were hurt and angry, but so was she.

"Lucy..." Her mother suddenly moved towards her. "I am so terrified — anything could have happened to you — don't you know that?"

"Oh Mom, I just thought I could take a break from everything, you know, run away to an island, just the way you said."

"I see," said her mother quietly, "but you won't take my advice on anything else."

"I didn't mean it that way," jumped in Lucy, "I just wanted to do something that would count."

"Count?" For a moment her mother was speechless. She gestured helplessly.

"Yes, count," said Lucy. "I want to make decisions... to change things. I *am* growing up."

"For God's sake, Lucy. This is not the way to grow up. I don't ever want you to lie to us again. And I don't want you to think that we accept stealing of any sort — ever. How could you?"

Lucy's face felt hot. Suddenly she could feel anger rising up in her throat.

"I thought you wouldn't care. You don't care about anything else I do. You'd like it if I went away somewhere so I wouldn't bother you!" Her voice was thin and high.

"Lucy!" Her mother's face turned grim. "That's not true! How dare you say that to me!"

"Why not?" shouted Lucy. "I never see you, I don't have any brothers and sisters... I'm alone all the time. All you care about is selling your lousy houses."

"How long have you been thinking like this?" asked her mother.

"A long time," said Lucy defiantly. She had finally said what had been hidden for so long.

"Well, it's not true," shouted her mother.

"Yes it is," Lucy shouted back.

"After all we do for you, you have the nerve to accuse us!" exploded her mother.

"Why not?" sobbed Lucy. "You're saying awful things about me."

"Lucy, we don't deserve this." Her father shook his head. "You steal from us, and then you justify it by saying you're unhappy. I won't accept it."

"We give you everything Lucy... your clothes... this home."

"It's the money, isn't it? You just want to make money," said Lucy fiercely, swinging towards her father.

"No, it's not," replied Mr. Fernandez.

"Well, then what is it? Why do I have to have dinner alone?" spluttered Lucy, helplessly.

"It's our work," said her father. "It's what we do. My job does take me away a lot, but you're fifteen, for heaven's sake. You're old enough to cope with that. I thought you understood that."

"No, I don't," cried Lucy , "and I don't want to. I want to be like everyone else."

"You're not different, Lucy. You're living in a make-believe world." Her father's warning struck very close to home.

"Well, I like it!" shouted Lucy recklessly.

"We don't… and I don't think you like it either," replied her father. He reached towards her.

"You don't want to believe me," Lucy said, backing away from her dad, "… because it gets in the way… just the way I do… I hate my life, I've lost my best friend… and I hate everything!"

"Lucy!" Both her parents moved towards her.

Almost choking on the hysterical tears pouring down her face, Lucy raced up the stairs to the safety of her room.

Lucy was lying on her bed with her arms folded across her chest and her eyes fixed on the ceiling. It seemed hours ago that she had flung herself on her bed. She was still in the same position. Downstairs, her parents were still talking, and the murmurs rose up the staircase to her room.

Lucy felt as though her entire body was weighed down. The ceiling spun overhead. She thought, will I ever get up and do anything normal? She didn't know what her parents were going to do. She felt as though they were downstairs plotting against her. At least they had each other. She was the person left alone.

She couldn't bear not knowing anymore. She had to find out what was going to happen. Lucy got up and crept out of her room. As she approached the top of the stairs, her parents' voices became clearer. She crouched down, one arm tucked through the banister. If she stayed very still, she could hear what they were saying.

"...since the shoplifting," her father said.

"But you know we tried, Jeff," said her mother. "I'm there most mornings, I sit with her at breakfast, I try to talk to her; but sometimes it's like talking to a post. She just sits there or makes some excuse about having to get to school early. I feel as if she doesn't want me around."

But I feel as if you don't want me around, Lucy wanted to say. She rested her chin on her knees. It felt weird hearing someone talk about you like that.

"I know," said her father. "She's done the same thing to me. But why would she get so upset about us not being home if she didn't want us around?"

"Oh God," said her mother, "the thought of

her alone in the Caribbean makes me sick to my stomach. Girls get murdered down there. And we wouldn't have known a thing...." Her mother's voice got thick and trailed off.

Lucy's father began to murmur, "Hey, it's okay, it's okay," and Lucy knew her mother was crying.

Tears rose in her own eyes. For a moment she saw herself, alone and frightened in a hotel room, menacing footsteps outside the door.

"You know, I really do love her," continued her mother in a shaky voice, "and then she's so aloof, or she pulls some stunt like this, and I just want to wring her neck. She can be such a *pain!*"

Lucy shifted uncomfortably. It had never occurred to her that someone might not like being around her. But hearing herself described like this, she had to secretly admit that it might be true.

"Yeah," said her father. "Well, we've never had a fifteen-year-old daughter before — maybe this is what it's like."

Lucy thought for a moment that she heard her mother chuckle. She could tell she wasn't crying anymore. She could hear her mom clear her throat and blow her nose.

"I guess it is," she said. "Jeff, I guess we are going to have to do something about being home more. I don't want to turn around next week and discover she's taken off for Paris."

"I've been thinking about that," said Lucy's father. "I'm going to talk to Dave next week about cutting down on the travelling. I'm not that keen on it anyway, and there are a couple of people who could take on more client work."

"That would be great," said Lucy's mother. "And not just for Lucy. I miss you too, darling. Sometimes I feel like we never spend any time together anymore."

There was silence for a moment. Suddenly Lucy felt different — maybe there was hope.

Her mother continued, "Maybe I can talk to the office about sharing clients — get rid of some of the evening hours."

"Okay," said Lucy's father. "But I think we've got to do something about Lucy, too. We can't just let her off. She has to pay back what she charged. Maybe we should dock her allowance. And what do you think about a curfew?"

Lucy gritted her teeth. She'd hoped they wouldn't get to this part.

"You know, I sometimes think she doesn't understand that you have to *earn* money," said her mother. "Maybe if she had a job...."

"Yes," said her father. "She definitely has

to earn the money to pay the Visa bill, and we need some other rules too...."

Lucy stood up. Her legs were cramped and stiff, but she didn't mind. She knew that the feeling of loneliness that had built up inside her was beginning to crumble. Why had she ever thought that nobody cared about her?

Lucy walked back to her room. Why was she feeling so confident? Just when she thought that nothing would ever change, something had happened in her life. The changes might not happen overnight, but suddenly she was hopeful.

There was one very important thing left. She did care about her friends. None of them had let her down, not even L.D. They deserved the same kind of honesty. Lucy tiptoed back to her room and shut the door.

It was almost ten o'clock. She tried L.D.'s number first, but it rang and rang without being answered. Lucy could feel some of her courage beginning to fade. This was also a very tough part. Nobody was going to admire her now. Still, she knew she had to do it. She hung up and dialed Erica's number.

"Hello," came Erica's voice on the other end.

"Hello," whispered Lucy.

"Who is this?"

"Erica. It's me," Lucy whispered again.

"I can't hear... somebody's whispering... speak up!"

Lucy took a deep breath and said, "Erica, it's Lucy."

"Lucy!" Erica yelled. "Heather, it's Lucy calling from the Bahamas!"

"No, I'm right here — at home," said Lucy loudly.

There was silence at the other end. Lucy could picture Erica's face. She could see Heather at Erica's elbow with her eyes wide and horrified.

"Lucy... Lucy, is that really you?" demanded Erica.

"Yes, it's me."

"What happened?"

"I got caught, but you know something, it's not all that bad," she added quickly.

Erica took another few seconds to digest this and there were some hurried whispers in the background. Then she was back on the phone.

"Are you all right? Was it awful? Are you in big trouble?"

"I'm all right. Yeah, it was awful, but you know, I'm glad I'm home."

"Is your mom there?" asked Erica.

"Yeah, so is my dad. He came back early. Actually, he's the one who found me."

"L.D. told us about your fight. She was

really angry, but she was worried about you too — so were we." Erica sounded a little indignant.

"I tried calling her. She isn't home," Lucy said apologetically.

"She spent the evening with us. Her dad just picked her up." said Erica.

"Okay, I'll try her again."

"You're going to have to come over tomorrow and tell us all the gory details. Or are you grounded?"

"I don't know yet," said Lucy. "I'll call you tomorrow."

She said goodbye and hung up. She knew Erica and Heather would be up all night talking about her. She dialed L.D.'s number. It was picked up on the first ring.

"Hi, L.D." said Lucy.

"Lucy, is that you?" L.D. didn't sound friendly, but she didn't sound really angry, either.

"Yes, it's me," whispered Lucy.

"What happened? Did you make it to the airport?"

"Yeah, but I bumped into my dad at the airport. And L.D., I didn't go with Clutch."

There was silence at the other end of the phone.

"L.D., I'm sorry about all the things I said. You're my best friend. I don't want to lose you," pleaded Lucy.

"Yeah, maybe I was unfair. But Lucy, I didn't want anything awful to happen to you."

"I know," said Lucy. "But listen, I'm okay and I've got so much to tell you. You won't believe it, but I'm so glad I'm home and not in the Bahamas."

"Well, you probably weren't going anyway." It almost sounded as though L.D. was smiling.

"What do you mean, I wasn't going anyway?"

"We read your horoscope this evening," said L.D. "It didn't say anything about travel."

About the Author

Nazneen Sadiq is an accomplished author who lives in Thornhill, Ontario. Born in Srinigar, Kashmir, in 1944, she moved to Pakistan after the partition of India. She attended Karachi University and Punjab University where she graduated with a B.A. degree in Philosophy and English. Sadiq immigrated to Canada in 1964.

Sadiq has written two other books for young readers, *Camels Can Make You Homesick and Other Stories* and *Heartbreak High*. She is also the author of an adult novel, *Ice Bangles*.